A Newport Christmas Wedding

Also by Shelley Noble

A Newport Christmas Wedding

A NOVELLA

SHELLEY NOBLE

WILLIAM MORROW IMPULSE
An Imprint of HarperCollinsPublishers

Excerpt from *Whisper Beach* copyright © 2015 by Shelley Freydont.

EPub Edition DECEMBER 2014 ISBN: 9780062362940
Print Edition ISBN: 9780062362971

10 9 8 7 6 5 4 3 2

Chapter 1

MERI CALDER-HOLLIS, SOON to be Meri Calder-Hollis Corrigan, stood on an antique wooden washtub in the middle of her grandmother's living room. The tub had seen many incarnations. First as the receptacle for Saturday wash days, then as a bed for several litters of puppies, kittens, and once a wounded fox.

For several summers it held geraniums by the front door, ice for the church picnic, and was even borrowed for a photo shoot for a brochure of one of the mansions Meri was restoring at the time. Today it was covered with a white sheet and served as a platform for the hemming of her wedding dress.

Meri couldn't help but fidget as Gran and Edie Linscott pinned and consulted and pinned again. Meri's mother, Laura, had worn this dress when she married Dan Hollis, and in the midst of Meri's excitement, her eyes would well with tears to think that her mother would never see her daughter wed.

She'd died several years ago, unleashing a secret that Meri thought would upend her life. It had, but in the best possible way. She was getting married to her oldest friend.

Meri smiled at Nora, her soon to be stepdaughter, who was sitting on the couch, hugging a throw pillow and looking starry-eyed. Meri felt a small frisson of nervousness. Stepmother to a seventeen-year-old. And thirteen-year-old Lucas. She'd know them all their lives. She'd even babysat them. But mother? She had no experience and the idea was a bit overwhelming.

"It's so beautiful," Nora said for about the fortieth time that afternoon and squeezed the throw pillow tighter.

It was beautiful, Meri thought. She'd stared at this dress through hours of fittings and never got tired of looking at the intricate patterns of the lace on the bodice and the edging that finished the three-quarter sleeves, just like she never tired of following the intricate details of a ceiling or mural in her job as architectural restorer across the bay in Newport.

Only, the dress was more special because she could feel her mother when she put it on. *Her mother.* Laura Hollis was her mother. Truly. If there had ever been a question about that, there was no longer. A frightened, lonely teenager had given birth to Meri, but Laura Calder Hollis was her mother.

The sound of a car stopping in front of the farmhouse had Nora running to the window. "More presents from Treasures. I'll go get them."

She tossed the pillow onto the couch and ran into the hallway to open the front door.

ALAMEDA WEBB OPENED the back of the white-paneled truck with her gift store, *Treasures,* emblazoned across the side. "Lots of boxes today. Meri and Alden are two popular people here about."

"They are," Nora agreed, peering over her shoulder at the contents of the van.

Alameda was short and muscular, what Gran called "a sturdy New Englander." She was certainly strong, Nora thought as Alameda shoved two heavy boxes out of the way, pulled out a long flat box and handed it to her.

"So Nora, are you going back to live with your mother after the wedding?"

"No. I'm living here with Meri and Dad."

"Oh?" Alameda placed another rectangular box on top of the first. "You okay with that?"

Nora nodded. "I'm fine. Why wouldn't I live with them?"

Alameda shrugged. "No reason. I just thought, you know, being newlyweds and all . . . though how nice of them to include you. Here are the last two."

She handed Nora the last two packages and closed the hatch.

"Can you get those inside okay?"

Nora nodded.

"You tell Meri and Therese I said hello."

"I will."

Alameda got into the truck, backed up and beeped the horn as she drove down the car track to the main road.

Nora watched her go. Suddenly her stomach didn't feel so good. Why wouldn't she live with Meri and Dad? They never said she should go back to her mother's house. They hadn't discussed it at all. Nora had just taken it for granted that she would live with them.

She didn't want to go back to her mother and Mark. But what if Dad and Meri did want to be alone? They could be alone with her there. Corrigan House had about a hundred rooms . . . well, only twenty something, but that was plenty of room for them all, Lucas, too, when he was home from boarding school.

Dad said Lucas could live with him, too, when Nora came to live with him last spring. But Lucas had this science high school he'd heard about, and it was too far away to commute. He sometimes came home for the weekends, when he wasn't working on some experiment or project or something.

But maybe that wasn't the real reason he didn't come back much. Maybe he didn't feel comfortable or didn't want to be in the way. Or maybe he didn't want them to get married at all.

Nora gripped the packages. She wanted them to get married. Her dad was so happy these days. Well, for him anyway. He never acted silly or laughed until he couldn't stop, it wasn't his personality. But these days he didn't go around all gloomy and deep all the time. They'd always had fun, even after the divorce when he'd visit on weekends, even though he never got to see them without fighting their mother.

These days he was much less . . . solitary. She'd even caught him and Meri singing in the kitchen one morning. Her dad never sang, he was the contemplative type. Or at least that's what Gran said and what Nora's psych book confirmed. Introvert. Plus, as a book illustrator, Dad did sort of live in his imagination.

They'd stopped singing when Nora came in. Meri said they had been arguing over the words of the song. Did Nora know them? She didn't. But they didn't sing anymore after that. Just had breakfast like nothing had happened. And Nora hadn't thought about it. But she remembered now. Would they have kept singing if she hadn't come in? Maybe they would have more fun if she wasn't around. Maybe they really would rather be alone.

Feeling sick, and suddenly cold, she turned to go back into the house. She went straight into the dining room and deposited the boxes on the buffet, where normally she and Meri would unwrap them and decide where to put them on the dining table, which was being used to display the wedding gifts.

Wedding gifts. Her dad was marrying Meri. Nora crossed her arms and pressed them to her stomach. When her mother married Mark, Nora and Lucas had lived with them, and look how that turned out. They started having children and made a new family. That left her and Lucas there, but alone. That's why she had run away.

But back then she had somewhere to run to. Here. Her home was here at the beach. Where would she go now, if the same thing happened with Meri and Dad?

"Hey Nora!"

Nora dragged herself back to the living room.

"There must have been a boatload of stuff. We were about to send out a search party." Meri looked down from where she was standing on the washtub. She was so pretty, and like her best friend. Nora was getting to know girls at her new high school, but Meri was always the person she wanted to talk to; to tell her about something funny that happened at school or any problems she had.

Meri stood there smiling, her dark hair piled up on her head to keep it out of the way, all thin and beautiful in her white dress. And suddenly Nora felt herself outside of it all, like a photograph that was torn in two, and she was the half that had been tossed aside.

"Nora?"

"Huh?" Nora rubbed her arms, trying to get warm.

"Are you okay?"

Nora nodded. "Four, no five packages. You guys are really popular."

Meri laughed. Her laugh always made Nora feel better, but today it made her feel sick. "Most of them are from Alden's colleagues and clients who won't make it to the wedding. You look cold, is it still freezing out there?"

Nora nodded. "I think I have to go." She looked around for her book bag and jacket, which she'd dropped somewhere when the bus let her off. She'd come straight here instead of home because she knew Meri would be here for her fitting.

"Oh? Tell your dad we're having dinner at seven tonight, because of the fitting."

"I will." She groped for her book bag and headed for the door.

"See ya," Meri called out.

"And button that coat before you go out," added Gran.

Nora couldn't answer. She needed to get home . . . wherever that was.

"THAT WAS WEIRD," Meri said, turning another inch and trying to catch a glimpse of Nora out the window. "Do you think she's getting sick or something?"

"Meri, hold still." Edie Linscott looked up from where she was kneeling on the floor. Edie was the best seamstress for miles and a friend of Gran's, though twenty years younger—at least twenty. Because though Gran always said she was seventy-something, no one had ever been able to find a birth certificate.

They didn't have birth certificates back then, or so Gran said. Not when you were born on a farm anyway. Of course, the subject of birth certificates was a volatile one at Calder Farm. Something that was never talked about.

"Gran, can you see if Nora got home okay? She sounded strange. I hope she's not getting sick."

Edie sat back on her heels. "Teenagers are always chasing moods. Highs and lows. When my two were growing up, there were tears and laughter, slamming doors, and the silent treatment, following so fast on the heels of one another, sometimes I just had to go sit out in my car till things calmed down."

"I expect she just wants to see Alden," Gran said. "With all the preparations and excitement, and with Corrigan House turned upside-down with decorating, she may be feeling a little unsettled."

"That's not good," Meri said.

"But perfectly normal," Edie said. "Turn."

Meri turned another inch.

"We'll have a nice quiet supper tonight, which reminds me, I'd better get the chicken in the oven." Gran pushed out of her chair. She was still spry and active despite her white hair and sensible shoes.

"Turn," Edie said. "I wouldn't worry about it. I saw Cora Miller at the market last week. She said she'd hired on as housekeeper over there."

Meri nodded. "We had to have someone. Between Alden working at home, and not the most aware housekeeper on earth."

Edie cracked a laugh.

"And me working in Newport. We needed help."

"Well, you'll love Cora. She was housekeeper at the Eddlestons' until they closed the B and B and moved to Florida. Craziness. But Bess's arthritis was getting to be too much. They wanted her to go with them, but Cora has family here. I thought she might retire. She living in?"

"Part-time to start. I think she didn't want to give up her house or rent it out. So we're starting with a flexible schedule. Mainly we just need someone to organize the household, do some meals, and be able to stay over when Alden and I are both gone."

"Which might be often, with you two working in different towns and wanting to spend some alone time."

"Alden offered to move us into a house in Newport, but neither of us really wanted to leave Corrigan House or Gran. But the commute can get long day after day. So we decided to keep my apartment in Newport for workdays and stay put here."

"Ah, these new marriages. You just make sure you pay enough attention to him so he don't go roaming like so many of today's men do." Edie shook her head. "Turn."

Meri turned. The only trouble with Edie was that she had opinions about everything, and always on the pessimistic side, except when it came to sewing.

Gran appeared in the doorway. She'd put on an old white apron with cross-stitched apples along the hem over her twin set and skirt. "Edie Linscott. Next thing you'll tell her is not to let herself go."

"Well, it's true enough."

"Maybe, but it makes you sound like an old lady. Meri and Alden know what's what." She pursed her lips. "Finally."

Finally, thought Meri. She'd loved Alden her whole life. It just took a while for her to realize that their love had grown beyond friendship into something quite different. And quite wonderful. She sighed.

"Is that a happy sigh or a had enough sigh?" Edie asked.

"Both," Meri said. "How much longer?"

"Five minutes. Therese, if your chicken is in the oven, come out here and be my second pair of eyes."

Gran carried her spoon into the living room and sat down. "Looks great. You can't even tell where you had to let the hem out."

"Good. I hate when things look altered."

"Which makes you so good at what you do."

"Yes," Meri said. "Thank you so much. I know it was a lot of work, but I really wanted to wear Mom's dress." She swallowed the lump in her throat. How could she be so happy and yet so sad at the same time?

"I'm just sorry she didn't live to see it," Edie said, struggling to her feet. "She'd be so proud."

Meri nodded; she couldn't talk.

"She would," Gran said matter-of-factly. "It's beautiful, and you know she's watching down on every minute."

"She is," Edie agreed.

Meri nodded. She just wished her mother were here in the flesh. She had questions. She didn't know many people who had stayed happily married. Dan Hollis had married Laura Calder when Meri was three. They were happy and would probably have grown old together if her mother had lived.

Gran and Grandfather Calder had been happy, from what her grandmother had said. She didn't talk about him much, but she visited his grave every week.

Meri loved Alden, she had no doubt of that. But she worried that things might be different. Which of course they would be. But *how* would they be different?

Would they stay best friends or turn into something else? Would they argue? A memory of Alden and Jennifer fighting, Lucas and Nora huddled outside in the yard, flashed in her mind. Would that happen to them?

"Okay, you're done." Edie stretched out her hand to help her down. Meri lifted one side of the skirt while Edie lifted the other with her free hand and her grandmother lifted the train over the washtub.

"Watch that you don't step on the pins," Edie told her. "I don't think I dropped any but my eyes aren't what they used to be."

Meri stood in one place on the oval rug while Edie undid the dress, lowered it to her feet, and helped her to step out of it. Meri reached for her sweatshirt and pants and put them on. Though the house was always toasty, she felt particularly vulnerable for some reason. "Wedding jitters," her friend Carlyn called it. "You'll get over them."

Easy for Carlyn to say. She'd never been married or engaged, as far as Meri knew. With no plans to in the near future.

Edie packed up her sewing box, and Meri and Gran saw her to the door. In the distance, Meri could see the lights of Corrigan House, a massive gothic structure that often stood dark and foreboding when Alden had lived there alone. Now, lights blazed throughout the house, thanks to Nora and, Meri suspected, Mrs. Miller.

She sighed. In two weeks Corrigan House would become her home. Alden and Nora and Lucas would become her family. Or she would be become part of theirs. They'd always been part of the Calder-Hollises.

And that's what made her breath catch, her pulse race, her stomach flip. Would it be like those scales of justice, balanced as long as everything stayed the same; but once the balance shifted, would they all come tumbling down? And if they did, would they be able to start again?

Chapter 2

NORA STOPPED INSIDE the mudroom door and shed her jacket and boots. They'd pretty much beaten the snow down into an icy path between Corrigan House and Calder Farm, and it had been slow going.

She was cold. Luckily the heat was going, the lights were on, and the kitchen was bright and smelled like lemons. Nora was still shocked everytime she came home to find that the living and dining rooms in the once gloomy, dark old house were painted white, the kitchen a light yellow. Her dad had commissioned it all when he planned to sell last summer.

Thank God Meri had put an end to that idea. Nora had been so grateful and happy then. Now, not so much. She wanted to be happy. But she was scared. Scared she'd be shoved to the background again. She guessed that meant she was selfish, just like her mother always told her.

She walked through the kitchen and opened the door

to the sound of vacuuming. Mrs. Miller, the housekeeper, was always cleaning. It should be annoying but it wasn't. Nora had loved Corrigan House the way it had been, dark and never dusted. It was always a relief to visit after her mother and Mark's perfect house in the 'burbs.

She hoped that Corrigan House wouldn't become like that. She'd never even seen the cleaning service from the other house. She'd just come home one day and find her room spotless and everything misplaced or thrown out, and it pissed her off every single time.

She didn't want to go back there. She wanted to stay here. She wanted Dad and Meri to want her to stay. They acted like they did, but . . .

Mrs. Miller looked up and smiled and went back to her vacuuming. Nora passed through the living room, the dining room, and out to the sunporch where her father worked.

He was sitting at his drafting table, facing the sea. Like always, he was wearing an old white shirt with the collar cut off, the sleeves rolled up, the whole thing spattered with ink and paint. He had graphics programs that he used for some projects, but he liked doing art by hand better.

He didn't notice her, so she just stood on the threshold watching him for a while. She'd missed him so much. Lucas had, too, though he'd never admit it. He was thirteen, out of touch with his emotions, probably. Or maybe he just kept them all bottled up inside. Kind of like their dad.

She moved in closer.

Her dad looked up.

"Gran says dinner is at seven because of the fitting."

"Great. I might just get this finished today, then."

"What are you working on?"

"A book of fairy tales. Like the world needs one more. But I'm not complaining. Job security."

"Which one is that?"

"La Belle au Bois Dormant."

"Sleeping Beauty? Huh. Symbolic, Daddikins?"

"Huh?" He stopped to look a question at her.

"She looks like Meri."

"Does she?" He turned back to frown at the picture. "I guess she does, a little. I've had Meri on my mind a bit lately."

He smiled and waggled his eyebrows, something he used to do when she was little and before the divorce had broken them apart.

"Well, when I get to the next story, I'll paint you as Snow White."

"I'd rather be Grumpy, or Dopey, or maybe Maleficent." She hesitated. "Or maybe you were planning to use Mom."

Her dad put down his pencil. Turned to face her. "I would never do that. Your mother and I weren't right for each other. If we had been more mature, we would have realized it earlier." He tugged a piece of her hair that had grown below her ears in the last few months. "But if we had, I wouldn't have you and Lucas. And if you're worried that the same thing will happen when Meri and I are married, don't be. We've known each other a long time."

"Since she was a baby."

"Yep. We've pretty much got the kinks worked out."

He reached for a pen. "Now let me get back to work. Mrs. Miller has been threatening all week to throw me out so she can start preparing the room for the reception. I don't dare stop. She might just move me out while I'm not looking." He made a funny face that made Nora laugh.

It was going to be okay. It was. It had to be.

MERI OPENED THE oven door and took a deep breath. "The chicken smells wonderful and done. Shall I take it out?"

"Yes, and then you'd better call over to the other house and make sure Alden isn't lost in his work and has forgotten the time."

"You know, between Mrs. Miller and Nora he's been on time almost always."

"I know." Gran slid the cutting board onto the counter near the stove. "But he's been distracted lately."

"We've all got a lot on our minds," Meri said. She picked a little piece of skin from the chicken and popped it into her mouth.

Gran shook her finger at her just as the back door opened and a rush of cold air burst into the kitchen. There was some stomping and rustling out in the mudroom and Alden and Nora came into the kitchen. Alden kissed Gran's cheek and handed her a bottle of wine.

Gran laughed. "You're a bad influence on me, Alden Corrigan."

He smiled and moved to Meri.

Meri's heart did a little flip, as it always did when he walked into the room. Tall and dark, thin but fit, black hair that curled slightly and touched his collar. Tonight he was wearing a black chamois shirt and black jeans.

"Just in time to carve," Meri said before he wrapped her in a hug and kissed her.

She wriggled out of the way. She still hadn't quite gotten used to kissing Alden in front of Gran.

And every time she reacted that way, Gran shook her head and rolled her eyes. Meri guessed she would get used to it. Alden had been her best friend ever since she could remember. He'd been there at her birth. They'd run the gambit of relationships, big brother to her little sister, brat to his teenager, mentor to her student, babysitter to his children, but always there was a bond between them. It took Meri longer to realize how deep it went and what kind of future they could have together.

Gobsmacked. That's what she'd been the day last spring when out of the blue she realized she didn't want to marry her almost fiancé, but wanted to be Alden's wife. She still sometimes marveled at how things had happened.

Meri handed him the carving knife.

He laughed at her with his eyes while looking totally serious. He always suckered her with that expression. She gave him a longer kiss.

"Better," he whispered.

"Yes, that's all well and good," Gran said. "But some of us are hungry." She poked Nora, who instead of laughing, jumped.

"Meri, strain the beans while I mash the potatoes. Nora, you want to get the ice water out of the fridge and pour?" Gran lifted the wine bottle. "I'll just get the corkscrew."

"You've created a monster," Meri told Alden under her breath.

"Yes, we have wild drunken orgies while you're slaving away in town. At least a glass each with dinner."

He considered the chicken, speared it with a poultry fork and began to carve.

Meri transferred the beans to a bowl and put them on the table, then eased the serving bowl between the bread basket and the salt and pepper shakers. "Nora, could you hand me that butter dish?"

Nora turned, her elbow knocking the glass she'd just filled. It bobbled then fell over, drenching the table and nearby dishes.

"Oh no." She looked around for a place to put the pitcher. Put it on the table and tried to pick up the glass and ice cubes. "I'm sorry."

"It's okay," Gran said, snatching a towel off the peg by the sink and tossing it over the spill. "This table has seen its share of overturned water glasses and worse."

"It's not okay. I'm so clumsy. I can't do anything right."

"Nora!" Meri said. "What's with that? It's so not true." She took a plate that had gotten the worst of the spill and tipped it over in the sink. "There. Like new."

But Nora just stood there, looking like she was about to burst into tears.

"You're very graceful," Gran said. "We're none of us

at our ease these days. It's bound to happen when big changes are coming. Good changes," she added.

An audible gulp escaped from Nora.

Meri frowned and glanced at Alden. He was concentrating on the chicken.

The spill was quickly cleaned up and the dishes replaced. Alden brought the chicken to the table.

Meri dropped a big chunk of butter on the beans, and Gran brought wineglasses for the three adults.

"Milk or juice?" she asked Nora.

"Nothing, just water."

Meri looked more closely at Nora. Was she getting sick? Was something bothering her? Something at school? Should she try to have a girl-to-girl talk with her after dinner? They'd always been able to talk before. But that might change, too. Being stepmother to two teenagers was unknown territory. Would Nora still want to talk to her?

Maybe she should mention something to Alden. Sometimes he could be so clueless, she thought, exasperated. Just as she thought it, he stepped behind his daughter and gave her a quick squeeze.

Okay, so not so clueless. Actually, to be fair, he was usually very with it. Gran was right. They were all a little on edge. Meri knew she was. Big changes.

NORA THOUGHT DINNER would never end. Gran had made her favorites and she barely remembered eating them. And to make it worse, everybody kept asking her if she felt all right.

Well, she didn't. But she wasn't getting sick. It was something else.

She went straight to her room when they got home. Meri hadn't come with them. She said she wanted some alone time with Gran. But Nora heard her tell Alden that he should spend some time with her, Nora.

She groaned and threw herself on her bed. Now she was a chore.

She didn't give him the chance to spend time with her. When the two of them got home, she said she was tired and went to her room. She even locked her door, not that he would ever come in without knocking.

He was good that way, not like her mom, who used to pop in at the oddest moments. Nora knew it was because she was trying to catch her doing something wrong. But her dad wasn't like that. He trusted her.

She tried to imagine Meri sneaking up on her. Searching her drawers and backpack for contraband. Putting her on restriction for her bad attitude. Taking her cell away because she talked back. But she hadn't done anything to make Meri or her dad angry . . . at least that she knew of. But that might change.

Especially if Meri had a baby.

Nora turned over on her stomach. *A baby.* Of course, they would want to have their own family. Then it would start all over. But she would be gone by then. Another few months and she'd be eighteen. She could get her own apartment. Or maybe she'd go to college. Then it wouldn't matter . . . except on holidays. But what about Lucas?

She reached in her jeans pocket and pulled out her cell. Opened the text app.

We nd 2 talk. Pressed send.

Waited.

Five minutes. Ten. *Where r u.*

Nothing.

Another ten minutes passed.

She broke down and called him.

"What? I'm busy."

Nora waited for him to bubble up from whatever thing he was thinking.

"Is anything wrong? Are you okay? Dad? Nothing's wrong with dad is there?"

Okay he was back. "I needed to talk to you. What if Meri has a baby?"

Silence at the other end.

"She's pregnant? Is that why they're getting married?"

"No. At least I don't think she is. But what if she does?"

"She probably will. And soon. Statistics show that second families are often in a rush to start again."

"Why do you know about marriage statistics? You're only thirteen."

She could hear him breathing. Finally he said, "'Cause I looked it up."

Then she got it. "You're worried, too."

"I am not."

"Yeah you are. You think they aren't going to want us around when they start having their new family."

"Well, they won't, will they?"

"Why not?"

A heavy expulsion of breath. "Haven't we already lived through that once? Mark and Mom did the same thing. Started having babies and revolving their lives around *them*."

"Oh. I didn't think you noticed."

"I noticed. I just chose to put my energy elsewhere."

Nora frowned. Her little brother was sounding like a jaded old man. "Is that a quote?"

"From the therapist they sent us to. Pretty good imitation, huh?"

"Yeah." *Too good.*

"So is that why you called? To tell me Meri isn't pregnant?"

"No, I just needed a second opinion."

"About what?"

"Whether they'll want us—me—around once they're married."

"You're just worrying about that now? Kind of late, don't you think?"

"So I'm not as smart as you. I didn't even think about it until this lady asked me where I was going to live when they were married." Nora sniffed. Her eyes were stinging and she wanted to burst into tears, but that would be such a lame thing to do. Especially in front of her brother.

"Well, think about it. They probably would like some alone time."

"They get alone time."

"Real alone time. Privacy."

"They have privacy. Meri stays here sometimes. They're at the other end of the hall. You don't hear anything . . . or anything."

"Ugh. TMI."

"Well, you don't."

"What if they want to mess around in the kitchen and you show up looking for a glass of water?"

"Oh."

"For an old lady, you sure are naive."

"I'm not. I'm just not like you, genius." And she was glad she wasn't.

"So is that all? I've got to study for my finals."

"What am I going to do?"

"Learn to cope. It's pretty much a done deal. And if you're lucky, they'll get a divorce soon."

"That's terrible."

"That's fact. Almost forty percent of second marriages fail within the first five years."

"Do you want them to fail?"

"I want to study for my test. I'll be home in a few days. I'm getting a ride with a friend and his parents. Now I have to go."

They hung up.

The kitchen? Why did her thirteen-year-old brother think about things like that when she hadn't?

But what did he know? He was just a kid who looked up statistics. Maybe she should get a third opinion. Not Gran or Meri. They would say that of course they wanted her, because they wouldn't want to hurt her feelings. And she would feel like such a jerk because she was thinking about herself instead of the wedding and how happy her dad was these days.

She could ask Carlyn when they went into Newport for Meri's surprise bridal shower.

Or she could ask the one person who would really know. She hesitated. Immediately got that familiar sick feeling. She keyed in the numbers and hoped no one would pick up.

Chapter 3

THE NEXT AFTERNOON, Nora went straight home instead of coming to Gran's like she had been doing. Meri heard the school bus stop down by the main road. She glanced out the window, only to see Nora turning into the drive of Corrigan House.

Meri had spent part of the morning with Alden and she was feeling happy and content, a brief respite from the anxiety and insecurities about married life to a man she'd known all her life.

Meri spent her days uncovering the past. Sometimes there were surprises, but basically a ceiling was a ceiling—for better or worse. A relationship was always changing. New discoveries and new understandings. Things had certainly changed between them. Something good. Deeper. She wasn't worried about the two of them. She knew they'd have their rough moments. God knows they'd had a few.

It was the other stuff that kept niggling at her. Could she become a part of their family? Father, son, and daughter? What would be her place there? Alden said he didn't expect her to play mother to his kids, just be there for them, as a friend, as herself, the way she had always been. When he said it, she felt like she could do it.

But now, watching Nora's pointed cap and ear flaps moving slowly between the dried stalks of sea grass that separated the two houses, she wondered. Nora had entered into all the plans and festivities with enthusiasm. They'd had great fun. Nora had gone with her and Carlyn to pick out their bridesmaid dresses. To choose things for the gift registry that Gran had insisted they have. She'd totally embraced the whole formal wedding at Corrigan House idea. Made plans to help decorate.

Then suddenly yesterday it all seemed to change.

Normally, Nora would stop to look out at the sea and the breakwater that guarded their little expanse of beach before going inside. But today she'd gone straight into the house without stopping, not even looking up.

"Do you think she's coming down with something?" Meri asked Gran, who was rearranging the gifts on the dining table for the umpteenth time. "She seemed awfully quiet at dinner last night. And she got so upset about spilling the water. Now she's gone home instead of coming here."

"I suspect she just needs some Dad time."

"Maybe," Meri said, and opened the package that had been delivered that afternoon. "What's this?"

Gran took the utensil from her, looked at the three-pronged claw. "Ice tongs. Sterling and stainless steel."

Meri smiled. "You mean when I'm married I can't use my fingers anymore?"

"Not for parties."

"When was the last time there was a party at Corrigan House?"

Gran sighed. "A long time, a really long time. But I expect having you around will make Alden more sociable."

"If you say so. But what about Nora? I'm kind of missing the old in-your-face Nora, spiked hair and all."

Gran placed the ice tongs alongside the serving flatware. "Well, don't. That was all protective camouflage. She's finally let herself relax her guard because she feels safe with Alden and with you."

"And you," Meri said. "And so do I." She gave her grandmother an impulsive hug. "You'll still look after us once Alden and I are married?"

"What kind of question is that? I should be asking that question." Gran paused.

"How could you even think we wouldn't be here for you?"

"I didn't. But I wonder . . ."

"About what?"

"If maybe Nora is feeling a little neglected, or in the way."

Meri pulled out a chair and sat down. "I didn't even think about that. I was so careful to include her in things.

But that was easy, I like having her around. I never thought— But of course all the attention has been on me, me, me.

"Ugh. I'm going to be terrible at this. And I'm not sure Lucas even likes me."

"Of course he does. He's just not around as much. And he's very much like his father."

"I know. Deep."

"Look at how long it took to break Alden out of that isolation."

"But Lucas is just a kid."

"A teenager now. But not to worry, you and Alden will see both of them through."

"I guess."

ALDEN CAME TO dinner that night—alone.

"She said she's not feeling well." He shrugged. "She came home and went to her room."

"Does she have a temperature?" Gran asked.

"No. I made her stick a thermometer under her tongue . . . when I finally found one. She didn't even know what to do with it. All of theirs are digital that read the temp instantly from the ear."

Meri looked at the ceiling.

"Well, I'm hardly ever sick," Alden said. "I guess we'll be shopping for state-of-the-art everything." He sighed, sat down at the kitchen table.

Gran poured him a glass of wine from the bottle he'd brought over the night before. "Maybe it just hormonal."

"She's always hormonal. She's a teenager."

Gran patted his back. "Maybe she just needs some extra attention."

Alden looked up at her. "You think that's what it is?"

Meri looked at him. She loved him so much, always had, but especially now. But suddenly she had doubts. Not about their love, but about what they were doing. Gran said it was normal to be nervous before your wedding. But Meri was afraid this went beyond nervous.

And she wasn't sure how to fix it.

She wanted to discuss it with Alden but he left right after the dishes were washed and put away.

Meri could tell he didn't want to leave. It was hard enough snatching time together with her working in Newport and him working at home. Add wedding preparations and family and it was a juggling act.

But they both knew he needed to be there for Nora tonight, even if Gran hadn't practically pushed him toward the door.

So Meri watched him trek across the dark path to Corrigan House, like so many times in the past. The moon was out and it cast the dunes and hillocks in stark relief. Alden's dark attenuated shadow moved across them in undulating waves.

Meri didn't stop watching until he passed from view and she saw a light come on from inside.

She turned from the window to see Gran watching her.

"Am I acting all gorpy?"

"Yes, at last. I was beginning to despair of you two ever figuring it out."

"What if everything changes?

"Everything will. Of that you may be sure."

THE NEXT MORNING, Meri packed up her car with left-overs for a week even though she'd be coming back to the farm Thursday night after work. She usually did since her boss, Doug Paxton, had put them on a four-day work week.

Even though Doug had scraped together enough funding to restore Gilbert House, they were still working four days instead of five. A shoestring budget was a shoestring budget any way you looked at it. And there were only so many sponsors in a whole town of deserving houses.

She kissed Gran good-bye and stopped at Corrigan House on her way to the main road.

Alden was already at work and she walked inside. For years the house had sat neglected while Alden used less and less of it. It had always been dark and oppressive. The heaviest of Victorian designs.

Its gloominess had never bothered Meri. As an archi-tectural restorer, she worked with old, really old, finishes and furniture, most of which were in worse shape than in Corrigan House. The project she was currently working on, Gilbert House, had been a boardinghouse for years, then sat boarded over and abandoned until Doug had "discovered" it and decided to restore it to its nineteenth century best

Since last spring Corrigan House had been transformed. Rooms whose dark walls had ascended into darkness were now painted white, the ceilings even whiter. The massive leather furniture had been replaced with a sectional couch in neutral tones with pillows made from South American fabric, red, blue, and turquoise, that "popped" —according to the designer.

A huge Christmas tree stood in front of the French doors that led to a patio and a view of the sea. The four of them picked it out at Addlebury Farm when Lucas had been back for Thanksgiving. The Addlebury men had chopped it down and delivered it fresh the following week.

It was decorated by a professional designer, keeping the wedding in mind, and Nora and Meri had made Alden take them back to the farm to pick out another "homey" tree for the family room.

They'd decorated it with found objects and popcorn and cranberry chains. And it was so successful that a texted picture to Lucas received a "Sick" reply. Which evidently meant it was pretty cool.

Meri passed through the dining room where the old family table still kept pride of place, but had been oiled and refinished. The buffet held two candelabra dug up from the attic and now polished and holding white tapered candles.

At last she came to the sunporch, which was also Alden's studio. It was another sunny day and the glass room shone with light. Alden sat bent over his drafting table. Meri stood perfectly still. She could tell by his energy he was doing delicate work, and she didn't want to startle him.

A minute later he straightened up, laid down the fine-pointed pen he'd been using. "On your way back?"

"Yep. I'm off to join the morning rush-hour commute. I just wanted to see how Nora was feeling."

"Okay I guess, she went to school. She seemed fine if a little quiet this morning. I don't suppose you have time for a cup of coffee—or anything else."

Desire shot right through her. "Nope. I'll probably be late as it is."

"Then I'll walk out with you."

She didn't bother saying he didn't have to. He put his arm around her waist and they walked back through the house, like a perfectly tuned machine.

She stopped at the back door and hugged him, hard. She could feel his heart beating steady if a little fast. She held on, trying to soak him in. Make them one. She was tempted to stay. She'd never considered blowing off work before. Not even when she was engaged—sort of—to Peter. But today she was tempted.

Alden extricated an arm and opened the door. They were hit by a blast of cold air. "Out. Before I take you captive."

"I thought you were working on a fairy-tale book. Is there a story about pirates?"

"Nope, and taking you captive would involve nothing suitable for the pages of Charles Perrault."

She grinned at him. *Really tempted.* She shivered.

"You're cold. You better get going."

He walked her out to the car and opened the door; just stood looking at her. "I'll miss you."

"Me, too. Maybe you could get away tomorrow night if Nora isn't still sick?"

"Tomorrow? No. I don't think so." He leaned in and kissed her. "But Thursday night you're mine."

"I'm always yours."

He smiled. "Always have been."

"I know. It just took me a while to figure it out." His breath was warm on her forehead. He kissed her and pushed her inside.

Meri drove away, watching in the rearview mirror as long as she could. He was just standing there in his shirt-sleeves like it was July instead of December.

This would be her life. Going back and forth between the work she loved and the family she loved. Living between two places and trying to splice it all together. Meri had never minded juggling acts before. And she knew it wouldn't get easier when they were married. But it would be exactly the right thing.

Traffic was heavy and by the time she crossed over the bridge and got off the main thoroughfare, she was craving another cup of coffee. Even when she was staying in town she only allowed herself one cup at her apartment and one when she got to Gilbert House. She did detailed work, a slip of the exacta blade and she could ruin a pattern or take off a finger.

She slowed as she passed by the front entrance of Gilbert House. There was still little mounds of snow from a surprise downfall a few days before. It softened the front yard—it was too small to call it a lawn—which wasn't due to be landscaped until spring.

But there was a huge evergreen wreath on the refinished door. Red holly berries were clustered in the curves of a red ribbon that laced through the branches and finished in a large bow.

The stained glass of the transom windows were clear and true to color. Hard to believe that in less than a year ago the door had been boarded over, gouged and splintered. The stained glass had been completely hidden and had to be sent out to have it carefully restored.

Meri drove around to the back parking lot. Parked and ran up the reinforced steps to the back porch where another door was hung with a wreath of pine, golden fruits, and partridges—plus one white dove of peace, compliments of the perennial volunteer, Joe Krosky.

Joe and Carlyn Anderson, the project's fund-raiser, hand holder, general magician, gopher, and Meri's best friend and bridesmaid, were sitting in the kitchen. It was a large square room that also served as lounge as well as boardroom; all their daily meetings were held there. It would be the last room to be renovated. Currently it leant new meaning to the term "green room."

"Slow day?" Meri asked, dropping her messenger bag over the back of a chair. She shrugged out of her coat and headed to the coffeepot. Someone had left a box of doughnuts on the cracked linoleum counter next to the pot.

Carlyn shrugged. "With colleges on break, we've lost a bunch of interns."

"You have me." Joe grinned. He was wearing his typical uniform. Overalls and a red bandana covering his orange-red hair. He was a Ph.D. candidate in microbiology at a local university, but he spent most of his days working on the restoration. He wasn't paid, and no one had ever asked how he could afford to go to school full-time and work for them full-time without pay.

They didn't know all that much about Joe except that he sang a mean karaoke, something Meri missed now that she was going home every weekend.

"So who put up the equal opportunity tree?" Meri indicated the miniature fir tree that sat next to the doughnut box. It was decorated with little plastic angels and was topped by a big cardboard Star of David that was listing to the side.

"We were discussing whether to do a manger and a menorah when Doug came in and nixed the idea of an open flame."

"Smart move." Meri adjusted the star.

Carlyn nodded. "And Krosky here said electric lights didn't go with the ambience."

Meri took her coffee over to the table and sat down. "Lord, I'm glad to be back."

Carlyn gave her a look. "Really? You'd rather be cleaning off old paint than spending hours alone with the TDH?"

Carlyn's code for tall, dark, and handsome.

"He's got a deadline, I have work. And there's not a moment's quiet around there." Meri smiled. "Well, a few. But not nearly enough."

"The voice of true love." Carlyn bit into a double chocolate doughnut and chewed. "So how did the fitting go?"

"Done at last. And it looks gorgeous."

Joe jumped up. "That does it for me. If you two are going to talk about weddings and go all squealy, I'm getting back to work." He bounced off down the hall.

Carlyn shook her head. "Crazy man. But he works hard for the money. Thank heavens he works for free."

"Did Doug come in today? Did he say when Hendricks is sending over someone to finish plastering the missing bits of ceiling? If we're closing up shop until after New Year's, I don't want to risk any more designs falling off and breaking."

"They're coming tomorrow afternoon."

"Good. What else?"

"The plaster casters left a message on Friday. The molds for the reliefs came out perfectly and they're ready to cast on a word from Doug."

"Great. Can we pay them?"

"Yep. That's where Doug is now, turning in projected expenses for the next quarter. There shouldn't be a problem." Carlyn looked up to the kitchen ceiling, which hadn't been cleaned or restored and still held the soot and grease of decade of cooks, good and bad.

"From my lips to the board of director's ears." She popped the last bit of doughnut into her mouth, licked her lips. "I've hardly had time to sit down for a meal for weeks. But now that the budget proposal is in, I'm going to enjoy what's left of the year."

Meri stood. "Just make sure you can still fit in your bridesmaid's dress."

"Not to worry. Well, back to work. I'll walk you down."

Carlyn and Meri walked out arm in arm.

"Goin' to the chapel . . ." Carlyn crooned.

They did a hip bump.

Krosky's "ba-bah-bump" echoed from somewhere down the hall.

"Gotta love him," Carlyn said. "See you for lunch? Kitchen at twelve-thirty. I'll send out for Chinese."

"I love Chinese," echoed from somewhere inside the building.

"The bouncing, singing, Chinese food-loving microbiologist," Carlyn said, and she and Meri bounced Krosky-style down to Carlyn's office, where Meri dropped her off with some fifties' hand jive

"And don't forget we're meeting Geordie Holt tomorrow night after work to discuss wedding pictures."

"I won't," Meri said, and continued on to the equipment room.

Chapter 4

NORA COULDN'T CONCENTRATE in school that day. She felt like a wedge was being driven in her heart. And it hurt.

She got up from her bed where she'd thrown herself the minute she got home from school. "You're being melodramatic," she said at the mirror. Her unhappy self just stared back at her.

She felt sick. The idea that they didn't really want her kept growing and growing all day. Until she felt like she might explode.

She wished she could talk to Meri. She could tell her things she would have never been able to tell her mother. But she couldn't, not about this. She had been naive enough to think they could be a family. That Meri and her dad would want her to live with them.

They acted as if they did, but maybe when they were alone they were wondering how to get rid of her. Lucas said they wouldn't want her or him. He'd been looking it up because he must be worried, too. He'd found all sorts of statistics to prove it.

Nora didn't care about statistics, she never understood them anyway. But her mother had said the same thing. And even after she had filtered out all her mother's bitchiness and the anger, she still came up with the same thing: no newlywed couple wanted a teenager around.

Even the woman from the gift store had been surprised when she told her she'd be living with Meri and her dad.

So why hadn't any of them just said so? She was a big girl. She could take it . . . sort of. No she couldn't. And they knew it. That's why they hadn't said anything. Because they didn't want to hurt her feelings.

What was she going to do? And how was she going to make it through the next week without totally losing it? She should never have called Lucas, and she really should never have called her mother. She was probably gloating over the mess she had made and was already concocting ways to make her life miserable when she returned.

If she'd studied more and made better grades she could have gone to boarding school. Nora groaned. She didn't want to go to boarding school. She wanted to live her with dad and Meri. Her mother had been right all along. She was a selfish, ungrateful be-otch.

THE GREAT THING about her work, Meri thought as she stepped out of the shower that night, was that you could take a long weekend and when you came back it had only changed in increments. Restoring a historic house was painstaking work. It had taken her nearly nine months to clean the paint layers from Gilbert House's foyer ceiling. Rush it, and you ran the risk of destroying a part of history.

Now she was in the process of exposing a triptych window that had been covered over with plaster board to divide a bedroom into two when the structure was turned into a boardinghouse. True to form, it also had several layers of paint—though not nearly as many as her ceiling.

It promised to be as exciting, if considerably smaller, than her ceiling. Because it was *her* ceiling, just like it was Joe Krosky's parlor wallpaper. And Joe and Doug's Edwardian fireplace. Each project became part of you, and you got very proprietary.

Meri dried off, then wrapped a towel around her wet hair just as her cell phone rang. She checked caller ID and smiled.

"Hi, Dad."

"Hi honey, back at work?" Technically, Dan Hollis was her stepfather; actually, technically he wasn't even that, but he was her dad.

"Yes, just for a couple of days. Doug's giving everybody two weeks off."

"Because of the holidays or the budget?"

"Both. Though I expect he and Carlyn will be working. It is the end of the year. And they have to file reports. So the rest of us are at our leisure."

"And how are the wedding plans going?"

"Whew. It takes over your whole life. I mean I'm excited and everything, though part of me will be glad when it's over so we can all go back to being normal." She hesitated. "We will go back to normal, won't we?"

"You'll go back to better. Trust me. My life was transformed when I met you and your mother. It may sound hokey, but it's true. I'm only sad that she's not here. She always had a special place in her heart for Alden."

"I know. I wish she was here, too. Have you heard from the boys?"

"Yep. And they're all ready for the big day. Will has even rented his tux. Matt is flying in on the Thursday before. I told him he better not wait until the last minute in case it snowed."

"How about Gabe and Penny and the baby?"

"They're driving, and Gran already said she would find someone to babysit during the ceremony."

"I don't care if little Laura cries and carries on."

"I know, but I think Penny would like to enjoy the ceremony quietly with her husband. She said to be sure to warn you that she's going to cry. She always cries at weddings, and besides, she's still hormonal. Though that information was more than I needed to now."

Meri grinned into the phone. Her dad was such a guy. "I just hope I don't cry."

"You? I hope I don't." He laughed. It was contagious, as always, and she laughed with him.

They hung up a few minutes later and she'd barely put down the phone before it rang again. Alden. The men in her life, she was so blessed.

"Hey."

"Hey," he said.

There was a second of silence. Like they were readjusting their selves to the new "them." It was exhilarating and scary. Soon she would add Corrigan to Calder-Hollis.

Gran had told her she could drop the Calder if she wanted. She didn't want to. Her dad had laughed and said she could drop the Hollis because she'd never get all those names on any official form.

But Meri stood firm. She was going to be Merielle Calder-Hollis-Corrigan because she was all of them and she intended to remain all of what she was. She blew out air.

"Long day?"

"Slow day. But wait until you see this alcove. I can't believe they drywalled over it. Though I'm kind of glad they did, because it looks like it's going to be in much better shape than the ceiling."

"That's good."

"You sound tired. Tough assignment?"

"No. Actually, I think I've crossed the line into whimsy."

"That should work for fairy tales."

"I guess."

"So what's wrong?"

"Nothing really. Nora's just . . . I don't know, not her usual outrageous, demanding, wonderfully funny self."

"Maybe school and wedding is taking too much energy."

"Maybe."

"Did you talk to her?" Meri asked.

"I tried, but she said everything was fine and went to her room."

"Well, it will be over soon and we can all relax."

"You wish it were over?"

"Just all the preparation. All you have to do is get your tux cleaned and show up. It seems like we've had nonstop fittings and tastings and—"

"You want to elope?"

Meri laughed. "No I do not. I'm just saying, maybe she's feeling the pressure."

"Maybe, but I wished you'd talk to her when—when you come home for the weekend."

"Will do. We'll sneak out for some girl time." Meri opened the refrigerator and looked inside.

"Was that the fridge? Haven't you eaten yet?"

"Yes it was, and no I haven't, but I will. First I just want to talk to you."

"About something specific?"

"Not really, just wanted to hear the sound of your voice. And ask your opinion. Carlyn and I are meeting with Geordie Holt for dinner tomorrow. You remember her?"

"The photographer."

"Right. I know she'll want to take pictures between the ceremony and the reception. They always do. But I also know you won't want to take the time, and she'll definitely want to take some outside shots, because she asked if we would be willing to freeze for a few seconds."

"She couldn't wait until summer?"

"No, she wants shots with the breakers in the back. It would be dramatic."

"I'll say."

She could almost feel his shudder through the phone. "Hey, we owe a lot to those breakers."

"We do. Okay, tell her it's fine as long as it doesn't take too long. Since we're only moving from one room to the other for the reception, I don't want the guests getting bored."

"What a whopper. You'd love for them to eat and leave so we can all kick back and relax."

"You're wrong, Meri. I want this to be the best, most memorable day of our lives."

And so did she. She was just anxious to make the transition as smooth as possible. She'd also noticed the change in Nora and wasn't convinced everything was fine.

Chapter 5

"WHAT I NEED from you two today," Doug said as he poured himself a cup of coffee the next morning at Gilbert House, "is a little housecleaning."

Meri frowned at him. "What kind of housecleaning? What about my triptych?"

"The triptych will be here when we get back after the new year. The point now is to get back."

Carlyn groaned. "Don't tell me they're threatening to pull funds again?"

"Not exactly. But it is the busiest season next to summer for the big houses. All those tourists coming to see the big houses decorated."

He looked over his shoulder at the counter Christmas tree and Star of David that had rolled onto its side. "I've got a dozen poinsettia arriving around noon. And fifty feet of pine bough."

"Why?" Meri asked.

"Because I have a contingent of people interested in Gilbert House coming in to take a look, and I want it to wow them. Well, as much as a partially renovated old boardinghouse can wow."

"Piece of cake," Carlyn said. "Right, Meri?"

"Right."

"So just do a little picking up," Doug said. "Give Krosky the vac and tell him to get up as much dust as he can in the parlor and foyer."

"They're coming today?"

"Yes, so chop chop."

"Talk about short notice," Meri groused. "And I was just getting to something interesting on my alcove."

"You're always finding fascinating things," Doug said. "That's why I'd hire you for life if I had the ready cash, but it will wait."

"And while we're housecleaning, what are you going to be doing?"

"Putting together a prospectus for next quarter for their reading pleasure."

"Yippee, strike while the iron is hot," Carlyn said, and jumped up.

Meri followed her example even though she had really been looking forward to getting two more days alone with her alcove. But sometimes finances were more important. "Okay we're on it. Carlyn, you spit, I'll polish."

By mid-afternoon the ground floor was in decent shape. Krosky had placed some high wattage lamps focused on some of the details of walls and ceiling and artfully concealed the bases and electrical cord with the poinsettias.

He stood back, hands in his overall pockets, bouncing on his toes.

"Heck, if I'd known you were so artistic," Carlyn said, "I would have let you redecorate my apartment instead of doing one of those DIY online programs. It did not turn out like I wanted."

"Next time," Joe said.

"I like poinsettias," Meri said.

"Me, too," Carlyn said. "They are one of the few flowers that don't make me sneeze."

Krosky stopped bouncing. "That's because they are not flowers. The red pigmented parts are called bracts, which are modified leaf structures. The actual flowers, the pistillates, are formed in the ciathia, those tiny little bulbs in the center, and are responsible for the reproduction."

"Oh my, I love it when he starts talking all risqué." Carlyn grinned and fanned her face with her hand.

"Well, it's true," Krosky said good-humoredly. "I like them, too."

Doug came in to give them a final inspection. "Looking good, team. Why don't you call it an early day? Carlyn has your paycheck, Meri. Krosky doesn't get one."

Krosky smiled and bounced.

Meri and Carlyn had often wondered if maybe he was independently wealthy, though he certainly didn't dress like it and he rode an old Harley to and from work, rain, shine, or snow. And yet he worked for free.

"I can wait until tomorrow," Meri said.

"I'm closing up tonight. There's no reason for the extra day when there are only four of us on the job. The heat is too expensive. Besides, you have a wedding to get ready for."

"Nothing's wrong, is it?" Meri asked.

"Nope. Not a thing."

"Then I'll gladly take the extra day off. But that's two whole weeks without my triptych."

"You can come visit it if you get tired of married life," Doug said.

"She better not," Carlyn said.

"But you'll come back to check on things, Doug. The humidity and the temperature."

Carlyn gave her a look. "Have you ever known Doug not to check on things . . . compulsively?"

"No, of course not," Meri said. "Doesn't mean I don't get to be a nervous Nellie. The ceiling is in a fragile position until it's repaired and gessoed."

"I will take care of it," Doug said. "*And* your triptych." He shooed them out. "Now go, have a good time."

"Talking about wedding pictures?" Meri asked incredulously.

Doug looked confused for a second, then said, "Why not?"

"Yeah, why not?" Krosky added, bouncing and grinning.

CARLYN PICKED UP Meri at her apartment at ten after six. "Sorry I'm late. Had a last minute number-crunching call from Doug."

"That's okay, I'll call Geordie and tell her we'll be a few minutes late."

"I already did. And there's a change in venue. She's was running late, too, on a shoot near here, so she said for us to meet her there."

"Where's that?"

"Our karaoke bar."

"Are we singing or planning wedding photos?"

"Planning, singing doesn't start until eight. But if we're still there . . ." Carlyn shrugged.

"Sounds like fun, but I thought about driving out to the farm tonight, since we're not working tomorrow."

"That's cool. It was just an idea."

"But nothing's stopping you and Geordie from staying. I can walk home. It's only a couple of blocks."

"Let's just seen how it goes."

They parked a half block from the bar. Probably the last free parking place in town until after the holidays, and Meri took it as a good omen. She was taking every little good thing as a sign, because truth to tell, she was a little nervous about getting married. Not that there was any question in her mind about wanting to spend her life with Alden and Nora and Lucas. There had just been so many changes in her life in the last year, it was hard to assimilate it all.

A gust of wind ran around the corner just as they opened the door to the club. They huddled inside. It was totally dark.

"What the heck?" Meri said.

A hiss of sound, a steady pulsating rhythm, filled the

dark. Ahead of them lights popped on, revealing the karaoke stage. At least ten people were crowded together on the tiny platform.

"Meri's getting married," they sang to the tune of "Going to the Chapel."

"And we're gonna par-ar-ar-ty." Friends, interns, associates, Geordie. Gran and Nora stood around the microphones singing and smiling.

"It's a bridal shower and we can't wait to get nau-au-au-ghty."

"Especially Gran!" yelled Geordie.

Everyone laughed.

Meri started laughing. "I can't believe you guys."

The rest of the lights came on. Two big tables were set with plates and decorations. In the middle of each was a centerpiece made of paper that accordioned open to make a 3-D LP and microphone. A buffet table sat against the wall, and additional chairs were arranged in a circle. Next to it another table was piled with gifts.

Ray, the manager, stood by the light switch. From the DJ booth, Joe Krosky, his hair reflecting the light in a red halo around his head, waved as he bounced to the music.

"He begged. So I let him come, but put him to work," Carlyn yelled over the music.

The adapted song finished and everyone piled off the stage, to surround her.

"Were you surprised?" Nora asked.

"Totally. Totally. How did you and Gran get here?"

"Dad drove us. He's picking us up at the end."

"He didn't drive back home, did he?"

"No, he's having dinner with some friends in town."

Ray passed by grinning. "Gotta go put out my private party sign. Don't want anybody crashing the fun."

"He closed the whole bar?"

"Until ten o'clock," Carlyn said. "He likes us, and it's a slow night anyway. So let's eat, sing, and be merry." She pulled Meri toward the buffet table, where Geordie Holt was pouring champagne into plastic champagne flutes.

She handed one to Gran and then to Meri. "Sorry Nora, you have to have soda. We don't want Ray to get his license revoked."

When everyone had their glasses, Carlyn raised hers. "To Meri, my best friend in the whole world, and to Alden, who better make her the happiest friend in the whole world." Everyone laughed and sipped, then broke into talking.

Music started up again from the DJ booth, Geordie and Trish Stevens, Meri and Carlyn's karaoke partners, dragged them onto the stage.

Everyone took seats around the tables.

The bass was pounding the floorboards. It felt great to be back up here with her friends. She'd missed this, Meri realized. She'd been too busy with work, and wedding plans, and spending time with Gran and Nora and Alden, to hang out with her Newport friends.

Carlyn took the mic and Meri took her place between Geordie and Trish. "We still have to talk about photos," Geordie yelled over the music.

Meri nodded and they began, "I Only Want to be With You," with Krosky singing the trumpet parts from the DJ's booth.

Everyone took a turn, including Gran and Nora, who really had a good voice, and enjoyed singing, unlike her father who had a decent voice but rarely sang. Meri smiled. A few times, lately, she'd caught him humming to himself.

They ate and drank, sang and laughed, until they'd made it through a repertory of wedding and love songs from Motown to Broadway to rock 'n' roll. Finally, Carlyn motioned to Joe to wrap it up.

While the music died down, Carlyn rounded them all into the circle of chairs. "Presents," she announced, and handed Meri a big rectangular box wrapped in floral paper and tied with a giant yellow bow. Then she sat in the chair next to Meri and pulled out her phone.

Meri gave her a look. "You're going to text?"

"Nope. A list for your thank-you notes," she said.

Meri nodded. Of course, Carlyn was ever-efficient, and she *was* the maid of honor. Actually, she had two, since she couldn't decide between Carlyn and Nora. Carlyn figured it out for her. "Hot Babe Bridesmaid and Hot Babe in Training Bridesmaid." They'd laughed and agreed and became HBB and HBTB.

Meri opened the card. It was from Trish. She read it out loud.

"*Aw,*" everyone exclaimed, and she passed it around the group.

As for the gift itself, she began meticulously separating the tape on the wrapping paper.

"Come on, Meri. At this rate, the last present will need renovating before we even see what it is."

Carlyn handed Meri a penknife, and she slid it through the seam.

"Perfect," Carlyn exclaimed.

"You're still not working on my wallpaper," Krosky yelled from the booth.

Amid the laughter from the restoration guests and smiles from the others, Meri lifted off the top of the box.

"Wow. This is great," she said, and pulled out a cookbook, followed by a crock pot.

"That way if you get involved in your work, dinner won't burn."

"Thank you, Trish. You know me so well."

"Look on the bottom."

Meri peered into the bottom of the box. Found another envelope. She looked inside. "A gift certificate to Chez Pierre."

"Just in case the crock pot loses the battle."

The next gift was a basket covered in cellophane. Meri opened it to reveal bath gels, loofas, oils, and bubbles as well as the softest towel she had ever felt. She held up the accompanying card. "To de-stress after a long day at work."

"I think she'll have other ways for de-stressing," one of the women said, and they all laughed.

"This is from Carlyn and Nora," Meri said as she read

the next card, and was shocked to find her eyes getting teary. She opened the leather book. *Our Life.* It began with photos from years before. Alden as a boy sitting on the couch surrounded by pillows and holding a baby. Her. Another taken a couple of years later. He was sitting on the beach trying to read, while she tried to take his book away.

Another package appeared between her and the book.

"Don't look at every pic," Carlyn said. "We'll be here all night."

"Thank you, guys," Meri said. "It's beautiful." She smiled at Nora, who was sitting between Gran and Lizzie Blanchard, who had restored the stained glass in Gilbert House and had take Nora under her wing and taught her the rudiments of glasswork.

"Okay," Carlyn said. "I've been told this is a bit naughty. From our wild and crazy interns. Close your eyes, Gran."

Gran closed her eyes and then opened one. Which made her expression take on a roguish wink.

"Nora . . ." Carlyn hesitated. "You can watch but don't tell Gran or your dad."

Nora looked eager.

"Joe, you stay right where you are. This is girls only."

Krosky made a rude sound with the music source.

Meri slowly pulled off the red ribbon tied around the flat box. Gingerly opened the tissue paper. Looked up. Everyone leaned toward her. She held up a red thong barely large enough to cover a quarter. Whistles and hand fanning followed.

Meri shook her head. As if she couldn't believe it. They'd be surprised to know that Alden wasn't always the serious, formal man they knew. He was a man who could appreciate a red thong.

"There's more."

Beneath, there was a beautiful satin teddy set.

"Something classy, something trashy," Carlyn said. "Now she's got all the bases covered."

"I think they're both very pretty," Gran said.

Carlyn took the box and wrote down the contents and the giver's name.

Next came a wicker picnic basket with china plates, two crystal wineglasses, and a bottle of wine.

A set of kitchen canisters and white designer utensils.

Geordie's gift was three picture frames that she explained were salvaged and repurposed from castoff wood and metal from Gilbert House.

The last present was from Lizzie. A wind chime made from delicate pieces of glass in Meri's favorite colors."

"How did you know I loved these colors?" Meri asked.

"You were wearing a sweater with them one day last spring and you said you'd just gotten it for your birthday and they were your favorite colors."

"Wow, and you remembered. Thank you."

There was a flurry of cleanup and more eating and drinking, though Meri switched to soda since she was planning to drive back to the farm afterward.

At ten o'clock Ray opened the bar to the public. The first one in was Alden.

"Am I too early? Should I go back and wait in the car?"

"Don't be ridiculous," Carlyn said. "You can help us carry these things out to your car." Meri handed him a stack of boxes. Nora went with him to open the door.

Some of the guests decided to stay. The others helped Meri carry the rest of her packages out to Alden's SUV.

NORA WAITED TO hand her packages to her dad, who was organizing the back of their new SUV. He'd sold the old Volvo last spring when he thought he was moving to the city. They still had his pickup truck but he said it was unreliable. What he meant was that he didn't think it was safe for Nora to drive now that she had her restricted license. So he'd bought a big SUV, big enough for the whole family, he'd said. But it wasn't big like Mark's minivan that sat six people and a baby car seat without a problem.

The SUV only sat four or five if you smushed. So maybe they weren't thinking about having babies right away. She wouldn't mind having a sister or little brother as long as they weren't spoiled brats like her stepbrothers.

But she thought about what Lucas said about second marriages starting families right away. And they both had seen what happened to the older children when the new ones arrived. They'd be shoved to the back again.

"Hey Nora."

She jumped. It was Lizzie Blanchard, the glassmaker who Nora had hung out with last spring. She'd even learned a few glass layering techniques.

"I'm starting a new class in basic glass techniques

after the new year. If you're interested, I'll make sure you'll get in."

Nora just looked at her. She'd get her into class? Nora couldn't believe it. She'd had really gotten into working with glass. Had even begun to think about going to college for about the first time and studying glassmaking.

"Really? That would be awesome. I—" She'd forgotten that she wouldn't be here to take the class. "I . . ." What was she thinking? Even if she did end up going to college, her mother would never allow her to study anything artistic. Everything was all screwed up. "Thanks. I really appreciate it." She swallowed her disappointment. "But I won't be here."

"No? Where are you going?"

Nora quickly looked around. Everyone else was busy loading the SUV or talking. "I'm going back to live with my mother after the wedding."

"Wedding" fell into a sudden silence. It seemed to echo in the night air. She quickly looked up and saw what she'd hoped she wouldn't see.

All conversation had stopped. Everyone was looking at her. Carlyn, Geordie, Gran, Meri, her dad. And he looked so—Nora knew that expression. It was her dad trying to control his hurt, his anger.

She hadn't seen him look like that for ages. Meri had done that. And Nora knew she had just ruined it. The sooner she left, the better it would be for everybody.

"Sorry. I would really have liked that." Nora left without waiting for an answer. She walked quickly to the far side of the SUV and got in the back. She slammed the door and hunched against the seat.

She'd screwed up everything. She could be staying here and taking glass art classes, instead of going back to live in New Haven. It was only a few months, they could have put up with her until then. If they wanted to. Which they didn't. They all heard her say she was leaving.

And no one had tried to stop her.

Chapter 6

ALDEN JERKED FORWARD.

Meri touched his arm. "Just stay calm," she whispered.

"Like hell I will."

"I'm sure she didn't mean it."

"Then why did she say it?"

"I don't know. But overreacting isn't going to make her feel like talking about it."

"Has she said anything to you about being unhappy?"

"Not to me. Gran?" Meri looked to her grandmother, who was looking at the back of the SUV, but Nora had slumped down in the seat, out of view.

"She hasn't said anything to me either. I expect she's feeling overwhelmed with all the preparations. Maybe a little insecure about where her place will be."

"Her place is here with me—with us," Alden said.

"And I suppose you're going to tell her so," Gran said.

"Of course."

"Just like that?"

"What's wrong with that?"

"It sounds like an order or a reprimand. You want her to want to stay."

"But why wouldn't she want to?"

"That, you'll have to *ask* her"—Gran emphasized the word—"and then ask her what she truly wants to do."

"And if she says she wants to go back?"

Gran sighed. "You know the answer to that. Now, I'll drive back to the farm with Meri if that's okay."

"Of course," Meri said.

"And you'll drive back with you daughter and try to have a conversation. A conversation," Gran reiterated. "Back and forth. And you'll do it gently."

Alden looked as if he might argue but merely nodded curtly, glanced at Meri, then walked around to the driver's side of the SUV and climbed in. A few long moments later the back door opened and Nora moved to the front seat.

The engine revved, the lights came on, and they drove away.

"Well," Gran said, letting out what might have been pent-up breath. "I hope you weren't planning on going out tonight."

Meri shook her head.

"I hope it wasn't the sexy underwear," Carlyn said. "You know how teenagers can be. 'Eeew. TMI.' "

"Maybe that goes for grandmothers, too?" Meri said, suddenly flustered.

Gran shrugged. "I thought they were cute."

Carlyn grabbed her and gave her a big hug. "You are the best."

Meri looked around the small group that was left. Saw Geordie Holt standing with Joe. "Geordie, we'll have to talk later."

"No problem. If it comes to it, we can do it by e-mail. I know what's what."

"Carlyn, can you stay here with Gran while I go get my car?"

"Of course," Carlyn said.

"And I of course will be here, too," Joe said gallantly.

NORA WISHED HER dad would just say something. But he just stared straight ahead like he'd never driven home from Newport before. It wasn't like he even had to pay attention, there was hardly any traffic.

And she was afraid to look at him, so she just looked out the window at nothing. Except for a few passing cars, it was like they were the only people on earth. She wished they were, then she wouldn't have to go back to her mom and Mark.

Well, she'd want Lucas there, too. And Meri, except she'd had them and now she'd lost them. Everything was so effed up.

And Gran. She should have asked Gran if she could live with her instead of going back to New Haven. Why hadn't she thought of that before she called her mother? That way Dad and Meri could have their privacy and she wouldn't have had to go back.

But it would make her dad sad to think she didn't want to stay with him. She did, but she couldn't say so because that would hurt Meri, and besides, she'd already told her mom. Which was so dumb.

Her mother didn't want her either. But at least if she were there, she could be her bitchy self and not have to pretend that everything was alright. Because it wouldn't be. It would suck.

"Why?"

Nora jumped and her forehead banged on the window. She risked a glance at him. He was staring at the highway like it was the most fascinating thing he'd ever seen. No, it wasn't that kind of stare. It was as if he hated every inch of asphalt. She hadn't seen that look in a long time.

Not since she had come back. Not since Meri decided not to marry Peter. Maybe, Nora thought, she was more like her mother than she wanted to admit.

"Don't be mad," she said.

"I'm not mad. I just don't understand. I thought you liked it here."

"I do. I mean . . ." Damn, she'd prepared what she was going to say, but now that it was time she couldn't remember how it started. *The kids*, she reminded herself. She took a breath.

"I like it here, but school is well . . . it's kind of boring." She loved school in Tiverton, she actually felt smart in the classes there. "And the other kids. Are kind of dorky." She *really* liked them. "I don't have that many new friends." But she loved the new friends she'd made. "I miss my old life." If she were Pinocchio, she'd have to let down the window to make room for her nose.

"I want to graduate with the rest of my friends." Except that she probably wouldn't even graduate because she'd be so far behind. Which would mean a whole extra year— No. She'd move out as soon as she turned eighteen, get a job. Never learn glass work or hang out with Meri and Dad by the water, or—

"You should have told me."

Nora shrugged. "It's no big deal."

"You don't want to spend Christmas with Meri and Lucas and me?"

More than anything. "There'll be a whole lot of stuff I have to get done before school starts in January."

He didn't say anything for the longest time. When he finally did, his voice sounded like it used to when he was fighting with their mother and was trying to control his temper.

It tore her heart into little shreds. She was so horrible. She should have realized the way things would be sooner and not waited until the week before the wedding. They would get over it. She might not. It had never occurred to her until she'd talked to Lucas that they wouldn't want her around. But she didn't have any questions now. *They'd heard her and they just stood there.*

They all heard her tell Lizzie she was leaving and not one of them said, "Don't go." She hoped her dad would say it now. And then she could say okay and pretend that she was staying because of him. But he didn't, just kept driving.

It wasn't fair. She tried to hold her breath so she wouldn't cry but she couldn't help it. She looked out the window and tried not to make any sound.

Until her dad reached over and put his hand on her shoulder. "We'll work it out."

Then she couldn't help it. She turned away from him and buried her face in the seat.

As soon as they drove into the driveway, Nora took off her seat belt and bolted for the house. She went straight up the stairs and locked herself in her bedroom.

A while later she heard his footsteps stop outside her door. His soft knock. She held still until she heard him walk away.

"I JUST DON'T get it," Meri said for the third or fourth time.

"No," Gran answered for the same number of times.

"Do you have any idea where this all came from? I mean we were into the wedding and Christmas and we were going shopping in the city and all sorts of stuff, and suddenly she's going back to live with Jennifer and Mark?"

"It does seem odd."

"Do you think she and Alden had a fight?"

"No. I just hope they don't have one now."

Meri sighed. "Maybe we all should have gone in the

SUV. I could have come back tomorrow or the next day for my car."

"I think the two of them need some alone time."

Meri turned to look at her grandmother.

"Watch where you're going."

Meri pulled the wheel back to the lane. "Am I preventing that? Is that what is wrong? Maybe she doesn't want me to marry Alden. I don't even remember why we were in such a hurry to get married. We could wait until things calm down again."

"Meri Calder-Hollis soon to be Corrigan, you're getting married next week. If you're getting cold feet, it sure had better be for the right reasons."

"Like what?"

"Like you don't love Alden enough to spend the rest of your life as his wife."

"I do love him, and Nora and Lucas. It's just— Maybe they don't need me."

"I dare say Nora and Lucas will do fine without you. Nora will be going off to college or a job in a few months. Lucas seems perfectly happy at his science school. But Alden? At the risk of sounding like something from your karaoke night—the two of you belong together.

"I've always known it," she added in a quieter voice. "Now I suggest we all remain rational and open-minded and not go off in hysterics, because chances are it's just a misunderstanding. And if it's something deeper, it won't be worked out tonight.

"Well have a family powwow at breakfast in the morning after we've all gotten a good night's sleep."

BUT MERI DIDN'T sleep. And as the hours ticked by, confusion turned into panic. What was happening? What was she getting into? She didn't even have a clue what Nora was thinking, and she spent part of every day with her. She just knew that the girl was so miserable that she'd rather live with her mother than stay with them.

She turned over and looked at the bedside clock. Another hour had gone by and still she was awake. She wondered what was happening in the other house. Had they worked everything out and gone to bed, forgetting to call her and tell her everything was back to normal? They wouldn't let her worry, would they? Were they even thinking about her?

She sat up. Pulled the comforter to her chin. Looked around the darkened room. Maybe she should just give up and go make tea or coffee—or even cocoa. But she might waken Gran. She eased out of bed and tiptoed to the window, careful not to step on the creaking boards.

The moon was waxing and it cast a cold light over the land, turning the dunes to mysterious shadows and the beach grass to sharp points and angles.

Corrigan House was dark. It used to be that Corrigan House was always dark. Even when Alden was at home, he lived by a reading lamp—not that he was stingy but because he said it was all the light he needed. He didn't mind the shadows closing in around him.

When things bothered him, he just retreated into his work, a place inhabited with fairy tales and nightmares, patterns and chaos of color. He was comfortable there.

But she wasn't. He pulled ideas from deep inside him and put them on the page.

She was just the opposite. She worked from the outside in, carefully uncovering layers until the past was revealed.

Maybe they were just too different to go through life together. Raise two teenagers to adulthood. Maybe have children of their own.

Meri reared back from the window. Of course. That's what Nora was afraid of. She'd said as much, not in so many words, but everytime she complained about the attention paid to her little stepbrothers.

Meri had always thought she would have children. Wanted children. Even thought about children with Alden. Maybe that wasn't such a good idea. But did she love Alden enough not to care about a family of their own?

Their own? Like Nora and Lucas wouldn't be theirs. But Nora was right. It wasn't the same, but that didn't mean she couldn't love them all.

Nora would be off at school in a few months. Would it still matter to her? She might even be starting her own family after a few years. She'd move away and only think about them on weekends. Maybe only visit at Thanksgiving or Christmas.

But what about now? Maybe she and Alden should have waited until Nora went off to school. But she'd seemed so on board until the last day or so. What had happened to change all that?

Meri rested her head on the window frame. The sky was just beginning to lighten. And way out on the dunes a figure rose. She knew that figure. Knew it so well, it felt like her own. And she could tell just from the way he stood that he was unhappy.

Lord, how many times had she seen him stand looking out at the waves. Angry, hurt, alone. She groped for her sweatshirt, pulled it on over her flannel pajamas. Found socks in the drawer and tiptoed downstairs, where she shoved her feet into a pair of boots left in the mudroom. Borrowed a padded jacket and hat from Gran and eased out the back door.

She wanted to run, but the ground was frozen and she had to slow down. She was close, no more than a hundred feet away, when he hauled back and heaved something he'd been holding into the water. He watched for a moment, then turned and strode back inside the house.

Meri stood there. She should go after him. Try to talk to him. But already she felt shut out. And what had he thrown into the sea?

She longed to go down there and make him believe they would be happy again. Like they had been a few short hours ago. But she was afraid she was the reason for what was happening.

Was she wrecking the fragile relationship Alden had with his children? Would she drive an irreparable wedge between them? She didn't want that. She would rather not marry him if it tore his family apart.

She turned and stumbled back to the farmhouse. It

was still quiet when she let herself in the back door and slipped out of the coat and shoes.

In a few minutes she was dressed and downstairs again. She placed a folded note on the kitchen table and again let herself out the back door.

A minute later she was driving down the car track toward the county road. She knew it was the wrong thing to do. Running never solved anything. But she wasn't running. She just needed to get away for a second. She couldn't think when they were so close and yet so untouchable. She needed some distance on what was happening.

Space to understand things, time to think things through, and most of all she needed to talk to someone who wasn't caught up in the drama, who had no other motives than to be a friend. After all, wasn't that what a bridesmaid and best friend were for?

She needed to talk to Carlyn. She could be back before they were even awake.

Still, she felt her world begin to crumble as she drove away.

Chapter 7

As soon as they got near Gran's the next morning, Nora knew something was wrong. More wrong then they had been the night before.

"Where's Meri's car?"

Her dad shrugged, but didn't look away from the empty parking area at the front of the farmhouse where Meri usually parked.

"Where is she?" Nora asked again when they got out of the car. She was beginning to panic, something terrible might have happened. Why had she ever started this?

She'd tried to do the right thing. Tried to think of somebody but herself, and she'd even screwed that up. Big-time. Like always.

"Maybe she parked around the side of the house," she said, answering her own question.

Her dad nodded as he walked toward the house.

"Or she might have run out to the market for Gran."

He nodded again, but Nora noticed he was walking faster.

It was everything she could do not to break into a run. Instead she crossed her fingers inside her mittens and prayed, *Please let everything be okay, please let everything be okay.*

Her dad was the first through the door. He didn't stop in the mudroom to take off his boots or coat, just marched into the kitchen.

Gran was standing at the sink. "There was an emergency at Gilbert House."

"When did she leave?"

"Early. I didn't hear her go."

Nora hung back in the mudroom, slowly unbuttoning her coat. She wanted to feel relief, even though it was bad if something happened to Meri's ceiling. But at least that meant that she hadn't left them. Only Gran didn't sound like she believed it.

"Where's Nora this morning?"

Nora stepped out of the mudroom. "I'm here."

"Well, take off your coat and hat and mittens and come have some breakfast."

Nora wasn't hungry. Actually, she felt like she might throw up. But she took off her things, hung the coat up, and dropped her hat and mittens in the basket on the boot shelf.

She stepped inside of the kitchen. "Did she say when she'd be back?" Her voice came out all weird, and Gran gave her a funny look.

"No, she left a note."

"Did she call?" Now her dad was sounding wary. It made her feel really icky. Like something even worse was going to happen.

"No," Gran said. "Nora, honey. I think I left the note in my room. Could you go get it please so your father can see it."

Nora went straight to the door. But instead of going down the hall to Gran's room, she pressed against the wall, out of sight, and listened. She knew they were just getting rid of her so they could talk.

Sure enough there was silence for a few seconds, then her dad said, "What the hell is going on around here? What did her note really say?"

"It said there was an emergency. I tried calling her cell, but it went to voice mail. It may just mean she's busy. But . . . I didn't expect this. I told her we would all talk about it in the morning."

"Dammit."

"Shh. I don't want Nora to overhear and be more upset."

Nora shoved her fist against her mouth. Gran thought it was all her fault. And it was.

"You need to remain calm. Women are bound to be nervous before their wedding day. And now with Nora saying she's moving out, I'm afraid Meri thinks she's the reason. And this is just a guess, but from what she said in the car last night, she thinks Nora and Lucas are afraid they'll lose you to her."

"That's crazy. They love her. She's always been a part of us. She's half the reason I got the kids back."

"Well, there's a lot of murky nonsense going on."

Nora heard the chair creak. Her dad must have sat down.

"What the hell happened?" Her dad's voice. "I must have been living in fairy tales too long, to actually think I could finally have my children and the woman I've always loved under the same roof. Silly me."

"Sarcasm doesn't help," Gran said.

"Then tell me what will."

Nora slipped away. Ran to Gran's room. The note was on the dresser. She sat down on the bed and read.

There's an emergency at Gilbert House. Have to go back. I'll call you when I know more.

That sounded believable. Maybe there really was an emergency. Nora folded the note and carried it back to the kitchen.

Her father was just putting down his phone.

"Did you get her?" Nora asked.

"I left a message."

Nora handed him the note. He read it, then just held it in his hand.

"Sit down, Nora, you'll have to have cereal this morning if you're going to make the bus."

"I'm not going to school. There's no reason to."

"There's plenty of reason to. Especially if you want to catch up with students back in New Haven."

"I'll be fine, Dad. I'm not going to school."

"I think we could all use a day off." Gran crossed to

the fridge. "And we're going to start with a healthy breakfast. Something tells me we're all going to need it."

"Gran, can Nora stay with you? I'm going into Newport. It's stupid to sit here and wonder what's going on. And I certainly don't want her to be away long enough to talk herself out of marrying me."

"GIRLFRIEND, YOU ARE totally nuts." Carlyn handed her a mug of steaming coffee. "The man is totally into you, Nora loves you, Lucas is away at school most of the time, and when he's here you get along, right?"

Meri drew her hands out of her jacket pockets to stir her coffee. They were the only two at Gilbert House that morning, so Carlyn hadn't bothered to turn up the heat. It was set at a steady sixty-two, warm enough to protect the renovation but not enough to be comfortable.

Meri had arrived at the crack of dawn to an empty house. She didn't want to go to her apartment. She didn't want to wake Carlyn up, so she'd sat in the parking lot alternately turning on the engine to warm the car then turning it off until it got too cold to think.

Not that any of her thinking was doing much good.

"I know Alden does. I love him, too. Totally. And the kids, too. And they like me, at least I think they do. But I don't think they want me to marry their father. You have to look at it from their perspective.

"They were treated like unloved stepchildren with Jennifer and Mark, and they finally come back to Corrigan House only to have their dad decide to get married."

"So you can all live happily ever after together," Carlyn said.

"Well, I think they may be afraid that they'll be stuck in the same situation again. That they'll lose him. To me."

Meri took a sip of coffee, put the mug down. "What went wrong? We were all looking forward to the wedding and now everyone is upset. If I'm wrecking the fragile relationship Alden has with his children, I would rather not marry him.

"Maybe it would be better if we just let things go on as they are now."

"And what are they?" Carlyn asked.

"You know, snatching time together when we can. Not making anything official."

Carlyn yawned and rolled her eyes to let Meri know what she thought about that scenario.

"That way they won't feel as threatened."

"You know, for a smart person . . . First of all, Nora may be a little self-centered, I mean she's a teenager for crying out loud. She's supposed to be the center of her universe. But she's almost eighteen and will most likely be gone in the next year."

"Which would be a perfect time to get married."

"Provided neither of you has been hit by a bus during that time."

"Jeez, Carlyn."

"Seize the day, girl."

"Would you do it? Marry someone if his kids didn't want you to?"

"Sure I would. I'd bulldoze right over them to the I do's."

Meri laughed in spite of herself. "You are so full of it."

"Well, did you two sit down and give them the blended family talk?"

Meri took a sip of coffee. "No. I mean, it never occurred to us. Nora's announcement came out of the blue last night. She might not even have told us if we hadn't overheard it."

"Yeah, that was kind of weird. Passive aggressive maybe."

"You mean she wanted us to know how she felt without having to tell us outright?"

Carlyn shrugged.

Meri's cell phone rang. She glanced at it, but let it ring.

"How many times has he called?"

"Three. Maybe four."

"Jeez, put the man out of his misery and answer. Tell him the ceiling is fine, it was a false alarm and you're coming home. It's not fair not to at least tell him what you're feeling."

"You're right." She reached for the phone. It stopped ringing.

Carlyn's cell started up with the theme from *Star Wars*.

Meri looked a question at her.

"Doug," Carlyn said. "I'll give you your privacy." She left the room.

Meri looked at the phone. Maybe she'd been hasty. No she hadn't. It wasn't just about what *she* wanted. They should all sit down and talk reasonably about what was best for them all.

But she was afraid that would not include her. Afraid that if she picked up the phone, he would say, My children come first. And they would break up, like she and Peter did. Though with Peter she knew it was the right thing to do.

Over the years, she and Alden had had their shares of fights and periods of being on the outs. But this would be the final one. It would mean she wasn't important enough to him.

Maybe it was better to get it over. She picked up the phone, made the call. It went to voice mail and she hung up, hurt and heartsick, but just a little relieved.

Carlyn came back into the room.

"Everything all right with Doug?"

"Huh? Yeah, just needed to check some figures. The man never stops working."

"Neither do you," Meri said.

"Well, I am taking the rest of the morning off. You and I are going for a walk."

"A walk? Where?"

"The cliff walk. Good for the body and the soul. And we haven't been in weeks."

"Because it's December and freezing."

"Well, you'll have to toughen up if you're going to end up a lonely old lady living over the deli with a hundred cats."

"You're so not funny."

Carlyn pulled her earmuffs over her ears and started on her gloves.

"Chop chop." Carlyn waited with her hands on her hips. "And if by some stupid reason you're still here tonight, I'll treat you to a burger at Mike's."

Meri stood up and followed her out the door. "You're going to freeze in that jacket."

"Not me."

"Carlyn, I'm really not up for this."

"Too bad. Sitting around all mopey and nobody-loves-me isn't good for the circulation. Now, put a smile on it." She practically pushed Meri into the car.

Carlyn parked near the Memorial Boulevard entrance of the cliff walk. "I figure we'll start here and stop for coffee when we get back. A little reward for our trouble."

"I'm not exactly dressed for the inn."

"Don't worry about it."

They took a minute to stretch, though neither was dressed for serious walking.

"Are you sure we need to do this? " Meri groused. "I'll probably get blisters."

But one gust of wind convinced her that the faster they walked, the sooner they would be sitting inside over double lattes and maybe a basket of pastries.

They'd walked for ten minutes, their breath huffing out in white clouds like old steam engines, when Carlyn suddenly stopped. "This was a dumb idea. I'm freezing. Let's go back."

"Told you so," Meri said, and then had to run to catch

up to Carlyn, who was speed-walking back in the direction they'd come.

That was fine with her, a double latte at the end of the walk was pretty strong incentive to keep up the pace.

They made it back to the entrance in record time.

And Meri saw the real reason Carlyn had suddenly changed her mind about walking.

"Did you plan this?"

"Yep.

"That wasn't Doug on the phone?"

"Nope."

"Not fair. You're supposed to be my friend."

"And your bridesmaid, and I'm not going to let you blow this because of some misplaced altruism which probably doesn't mean squat. Now you tell the man exactly what you're feeling and why, and for crying out loud, try to work things out.

"This is the first bridesmaid dress I've ever had that actually looks good on me, and I intend to wear it." She veered off the path and with a quick wave cut across the lawn to the parking lot.

And Meri was left looking at the uncompromising face of her hopefully soon-to-be bridegroom.

Chapter 8

MERI DIDN'T HESITATE, but walked toward him. She'd thought she'd need time and space to sort things out, but just seeing him told her everything she already knew. All that cornball stuff about a person being the other half of you, of completing you. It was true.

She hadn't known before that there was a little emptiness inside her. If she ever questioned it, she thought it was because of her birth. But now she knew. That piece she needed was standing right in front of her.

And she walked into his arms like she had hundreds of times before. For thirty years she'd been coming home and she never realized it fully. Not even the past summer, when she finally admitted that she loved him, was in love with him.

His arms closed around her. No questions, just acceptance. Like always. She knew she owed him an explanation, and that would come soon enough, but for now she held on for dear life.

"There was no emergency at Gilbert House."

"No," she said into his jacket.

"Didn't think so."

They stood on the path while time winked out, until Alden rested his cheek on her hair. "Can we go home now?"

Meri just wanted to stand there. But that was crazy. "I love you totally, but I'm . . . I'm . . ."

"Afraid."

Of course he knew. She nodded.

"Can we at least go inside, my ears are turning to popsicles."

Meri chuckled. "Coffee at my place?"

MERI LET THEM inside. They'd been pretty much silent on the ride to her apartment. It never did any good to try to talk to Alden when he was driving or working. And what she needed to say, needed to ask, deserved face-to-face time.

And since Alden was never chatty at the best of times, she spent the time looking out the window of decorated Newport. Normally, she relished driving through the town at Christmastime. The town was at its festive best and the streets were crowded with visitors coming to see the mansions all decked out.

She always went to at least one every year. The mansions, when decorated, went a step further than just the return of a certain age. They showed the possibility, the human element, that was sometimes missing in the daily tours.

The people who built these mansions might not always have been the nicest or most sympathetic of people. But they celebrated and grieved just like everyone else.

That's what she liked about Gilbert House. It would never be as fabulous as the Breakers, or Rosecliff or Marble House. It was smaller, earlier, and had seen many generations of people from all walks of life. You could feel their presence in the very wood and tile of the house. Could walk the same steps as someone over a hundred years before. It was neat. She loved it.

That's the first thing she and Alden had talked about when they decided to get married.

How would they juggle two households, because she intended to work.

It had never occurred to him that she wouldn't work. She glanced over at his stark profile, eyes forward and mind who knew where. On the traffic, probably—or in some dark cavern or aerie fairy palace.

She loved him so much. He was such a part of her that she couldn't imagine life without him. Well, she'd never had to, had she? He'd always been there. He'd been all things to her during her thirty years and now he would be her husband—or not.

She closed her eyes, leaned her head back against the headrest.

"Tired?"

"I didn't sleep much."

"Strange, neither did I."

"I know."

He cut a look at her before retuning to the street.

"I saw you out on the rocks," she said.

"Why didn't you come to me instead of hying off to Newport?"

"I don't know. You looked so angry. And I didn't know what to say or how to fix it."

"I wasn't angry. Okay maybe I was angry, but not at you."

"At Nora?"

"I'm a little pissed at Nora. Mainly I was just angry at the fates that were suddenly playing fast and loose with our future."

Meri smiled at him.

"I know, I think I'm a little crazy, too."

"You're not crazy at all. You're the love of my life. Look, someone's coming out of a space up there."

"Miracle of miracles. I wasn't relishing driving around forever trying to find a parking space while trying not to start a conversation until we could just talk with no inter-ruptions."

"Me neither."

He pulled alongside the recently vacated spot and backed in.

"Pretty impressive how you squeezed this big car into that little space."

"I had incentive."

"Coffee?"

He shook his head, amused. "Get out."

They walked up the sidewalk arm in arm, and if Meri's stomach hadn't been bouncing around like a free radical, she would have enjoyed the walk.

Though she did calm down as they turned into her apartment building , an old house converted into apartments that was in walking distance of just about everything but the mansions.

As soon as they were inside, Alden threw his jacket on the couch arm and went into her little kitchen to make coffee. Meri began to get nervous again. Usually he hung his coat up in the closet, so maybe he just really needed coffee. Or was he planning for a quick getaway?

Meri picked it up and hung up both their coats. She came up behind him and put her arms around his waist while he watched the coffee carafe.

"I'm taking it that it isn't me you're upset with?" he asked.

She rested her head against his back. "I'm not upset at anyone. Just suddenly I'm not sure about what we're doing."

He turned and put both arms around her. "Because Nora wants to go live with her mother?"

"Why? She never said anything about it. I thought she was totally on board with the wedding. She's been over at Gran's every day making plans. We were going shopping on Saturday. What happened?"

The coffee beeped and he got two mugs down from the cabinet. "She said it was no big deal, that school was boring and she wanted to graduate with her friends in New Haven."

"Did you believe her?"

"Not really, but why else would she want to go home? She knows you and I and Gran love her and want her here."

"Are you sure she knows?"

"Aren't you?"

"No," Meri said. "I'm not sure of anything suddenly. Here Nora is suddenly leaving home, and I think it's because of me."

"Don't be ridiculous. She loves you."

"As somebody she hangs out with occasionally. But what about being like a parent? What if I mess up? She could have told me what was bothering her but she didn't. What if she needs help and I miss the cues. And—"

"Stop it." He had been about to hand her a mug, but put it down on the counter. Took her shoulders, squeezed them. "You don't have to be a mother. To Nora or Lucas or even to whatever might come down the road. And Nora is smart enough to know we both love her."

"Now maybe, but what if they come to resent me for taking you away from them?"

"What kind of television have you been watching?"

"I just don't want to come between the three of you. They've lived so long without you, now Nora's willing to go back to a place she hated, what else could it be? Why didn't I just ask her what she was feeling? I just took it for granted she was as happy as I was."

"She was. I'm sure of it."

"Then what happened? What did she say last night?"

"What I just told you about school, and she refused to go to school today. I didn't argue but left her with Gran. Maybe she'll talk some sense into her."

"What about Lucas, he hasn't even been around?"

"He'll cope, he always does. He was fine with it when we told him. Later, he told me he thought it was a good idea, since Nora would be leaving soon and he thought I should have someone to keep me company. I felt ancient." He smiled slowly. "For about a second, then, I thought of you keeping me company and I was myself again."

"Maybe we should just stay like we are."

"And what is that?"

"You know . . . this."

"Standing in your kitchen while our coffee gets cold listening to you talking nonsense?"

"It doesn't feel like nonsense."

"I know. I didn't mean to make light of it. I've waited my whole life to have my family together. And now I'm close. I'm nervous, too."

"I'm not even your family."

"Of course you are. I knew from the moment I saw you that you were mine." He grinned. "Those pink little toes, that soft baby bum."

"Stop it." He made her laugh, and this was too serious to laugh about.

"Now it's just a question of making it legal."

"But what if it isn't even legal?"

"Dammit, Meri. Are you looking for impediments?

It's legal enough for me. But if you're looking for a way out, just say so."

"No. I'm not. I just want it to be perfect."

He huffed out a sigh. "Right now, I just want it to be. Come on, you've never been a fraidy cat before."

She felt a smile start but wasn't sure it if would lead to laughter or tears. "What if we end up getting a divorce and hate each other?"

"We've had fights before, we've always found our way back, we will again."

"But—"

Alden moved away. "No more buts. Either you love me and want to marry me or you don't. You decide. But Meri, this is it. If you decide you don't want me, it's forever. I won't be coming back. I'm finished with waiting."

She stared at him.

He brushed past her, went straight to the coat closet and yanked his coat off the hanger.

Meri found her voice. "Alden. Stop. What are you doing?" She hurried toward him, but he already had his hand on the doorknob.

"Alden, you know I love you."

"Then make a decision."

"But what about Nora?"

He didn't answer, just opened the door, then slammed it as he left.

"WHERE IS HE? Why aren't they answering their phones?" Nora placed her own cell phone on the kitchen table and stared at it. She felt like breaking the stupid thing, but it cost big bucks and maybe Meri or her dad would call. It was already dark and no one had called.

"Gran? Can't you do something?"

Gran shook her head. "It's in their hands. But I think you should tell your dad what you've told me."

Nora crossed her arms on the table and buried her head. "I should never have come. He was happy until I showed up."

"Nora. Cut this nonsense out at once. You're not responsible for anything except having really poor timing and not trusting your father and Meri enough to tell them what your fears were."

Nora peered up at Gran. "I was trying to do the right thing."

"I know you were. You were going to sacrifice living here so you wouldn't be in the way. And the fact that you could even think that way makes me want to smack your mother. Though I know I shouldn't say that. But so help me she makes me angry.

"And furthermore you won't be going back there at any cost. Consequences indeed. You can live here if you don't want to live with Meri and Alden, but you're not going back to that house."

"But I really do want to live with Dad and Meri."

"Then tell them so."

"What if it's too late?" Nora waited for Gran to tell her that it was never too late to make things right, but she didn't. She didn't say anything.

Gran was looking out the window. "If it is, we'll think of something else."

Just then a light flashed in the through the window. They both ran to the kitchen door. The SUV was bouncing over the track that led to the farm.

"Do you see Meri? Is she with him?"

Gran craned her neck. "I can't see. Go sit down. And stay calm."

"You don't see her, do you?"

"Nora, sit down and control yourself. We've had quite enough excitement for one day."

It took forever before Nora heard the car door slam, the back door open and close. And her dad walked in—alone.

Nora forgot she was supposed to be calm.

"Where is she?"

"In Newport."

Gran reached into the cabinet and brought out a wineglass that she filled and put on the table. She kept her eyes on Alden.

"Why didn't she come back?"

"She said she needed to think."

"It's because of me saying I was going to live with mom, isn't it?"

"That was just the catalyst."

"I'm sorry." She glanced at Gran.

"Go on and tell him what you told me."

"I don't want to live in New Haven."

"Then why the hell did you—"

"Alden, listen to your daughter, and hear her out before you interrupt again."

Alden sat down, laced his fingers and rested his hands on the kitchen table like a dutiful student.

"People kept asking me if I would be going back to Mom after you and Meri got married. They thought it was weird that you'd want me to stay."

"What people?"

"Alameda from the gift shop, and some of the girls at the shower were surprised that I was staying. They all thought you two would want to be alone."

"For Chr—"

"Alden." Gran shook her finger at him.

"So I called Lucas and he had all these statistics about . . . stuff. You know, like divorces and starting new families, and he said it would be just like living with Mark and Mom once you and Meri . . . got married and started—" She blushed, she couldn't help it. "You know. Your own family. Lucas doesn't act like he's living in this world, but he is, and he's a lot smarter than I am."

"So Lucas doesn't want us to get married?"

Nora frowned. "He didn't say that. He just said what would happen. And I know I'll be going to college or something soon, and I wouldn't have said anything until after the wedding because I don't want to mess up things between you and Meri, but Lizzie from the glass studio had saved me a place in her glass class for next semester and I didn't think it was fair not to tell her. I didn't think anyone would hear."

"Why didn't you just ask us?" Alden said.

"I would have, but I didn't want to be ungrateful."

"Ungrateful?"

"That you took me in."

"What? Nora, you're my daughter, this is your home. Where the hell did you get that idea?"

"Well, I wasn't thinking too straight. I wanted to ask Gran but I knew she would tell me I was wanted, because she'd have to."

Gran held up her hand to Alden. "I've already straightened her out on that point."

"So I—now don't get mad—I called Mom."

"What?" Alden reared up from his seat, but Gran pushed him back down.

"I didn't know what else to do." Nora's voice rose until the last words were like a plea.

Alden shot his fingers through his hair. "I should have recognized her hand in this mess. You couldn't just ask me?"

"I know you would want me to stay. And I'm pretty sure Meri would want me to stay. But Mom said there's no room for teenagers in a new marriage. And that I would be in the way. And she said I was an ungrateful, spoiled girl and I could come back, but there would be consequences." Nora's face twisted and she started to cry. "But I didn't care. It would only be until I turned eighteen and then I could move out and she couldn't stop me."

Alden leaned back in his chair and rubbed his face with both hands.

"Don't be mad," she begged. "I know I've ruined everything. I'll pack and leave today. Just tell Meri to come back."

Her dad's shoulders began to shake. She'd never seen him cry before, ever.

"Daddy," she wailed. "Please don't be sad."

He shook his head and uncovered his face.

He wasn't crying, he was laughing, but not the funny kind of laughing. "What did I do in a former life to deserve two such remarkable, infuriating women that I can't live without?"

Nora stared.

Gran smiled.

Alden pulled himself together.

"You'll go get her and make her come home?" Nora asked.

"No."

"But Dad—"

"Nora, I brought your mother here against her will. I thought she would get to like it here, but she didn't. I won't make the same mistake with Meri."

"But Meri loves it here."

"She'll come to her decision without us."

"But what if it's the wrong decision?"

"Then we'll all learn to live with it."

Chapter 9

MERI HAD TRIED to pull herself together before meeting Carlyn at their favorite pub for dinner. Hopefully, she looked better than she felt.

She still couldn't believe that Alden drove all this way and then just left before they had a chance to really talk things out.

It was still early when she set out for Mike's. The pub was only a few blocks away, and Meri decided to walk. She'd been spending so much time out at the farm and working that she hadn't had a chance to enjoy Newport at its most festive.

The houses were draped in pine boughs and wreaths. Candles lit every window. Store windows were trimmed in lights and greenery. Happy. This was a happy season. A season of fruition and celebration of the new. A time of promise. Of hope.

She had thought it was the perfect time for a wedding,

the changing of one life and joining with another. A perfect time. Until the bridal shower.

And it wasn't just Nora. If that was the only issue, Meri would have sat her down and they would have talked it out.

No. Nora's defection had unleashed all the ifs that Meri had refused to look at before. Things she wasn't sure of. And now Alden had given her an ultimatum. She knew Alden. Understood now that he'd wanted this all along. And now she had to decide or lose him forever. It would have sounded corny coming from anyone else. But not Alden.

He'd been patient with her, waited for her to grow up, stood back while she created her own life and had loved her unconditionally all the while.

How could she ever live up to his expectations?

MIKE'S WAS A small neighborhood bar in the basement of a white clapboard federal house circa 1774. The basement window was framed in colored lights with a dancing Santa standing on the ledge.

Meri opened the heavy wooden door and stepped into the bar. The jukebox played oldies and Irish folk songs, depending on the crowd. Tonight it was playing something slow, mournful, sung by a fine tenor voice with a harp as accompaniment.

And she'd been hoping for something a little more lively, like "Jingle Bell Rock."

Carlyn was sitting in a booth against the far wall. The

place was pretty crowded, but the music had a subduing affect, so Mike McGee's welcome had everyone turning around and looking to see who had come in.

Meri waved back, ducked her head and hurried across the room to slide into the booth opposite Carlyn. There were two glasses of red wine on the table.

"Girlfriend, you look like shit. I really didn't think you'd be here for dinner."

"That's okay, I'll pay for my own burger."

"That's not what I mean." Carlyn lifted her hand and a waitress wearing felt reindeer antlers came over to the table.

They ordered their usual giant cheese burgers, juicy and fire grilled, and an order of onion rings to share. "To round out the vegetable pyramid," Carlyn said. "Now tell me what happened? Or should I ask what didn't happen?"

Meri took a sip of wine. She hadn't eaten all day and it set off a burning in her stomach. Great, she was probably giving herself an ulcer over all this.

"Well?"

"We went back to my apartment."

"Good," Carlyn said. "That's good, right?"

"He made coffee."

"Oo-kay. And?"

"We were standing there, and everything seemed fine, but then we started talking and I told him all the stuff I was worried about. Like Nora, and how everything might change, and other stuff. And he was all like fine and saying it would be okay. And then—"

Meri thought back. She'd spent the afternoon thinking about that final exit. "I said something about what if we ended up hating each other and getting a divorce."

"Oh Lord, Meri. That's the chance you take. It's called life. What did he say to that?"

"He told me to make up my mind and whatever I decided would be that—forever."

"What? I totally didn't understand that."

"He said—" She really didn't want to share this, even with Carlyn. But she needed Carlyn's down-to-earth perspective. And besides, they were best friends. "He said either I loved him or didn't and I had to decide. But that if I decided I didn't want him, it would be forever. Or something like that—I was so stunned. Then he said he was finished with waiting. And he turned around and left."

"Criminy." Carlyn leaned across the table. "And you let him go?"

"How could I stop him?"

"By saying 'I love you madly, of course I want to get married. Can't wait.' "

Meri hid her face in her hands. Shook her head. "I am so stupid."

"Pretty much, if you're here having burgers with me and not with Alden."

The waitress brought their burgers and set the plate of onion rings between them.

The sight of them made Meri queasy.

Carlyn slid the mustard toward her.

"What am I going to do?"

"You're asking me?" Carlyn shook catsup onto her plate. "Ms. Cut and Run?"

"Well, you're the best I've got."

Carlyn grinned. "I think there's a song about that."

"Don't you dare. I'm on the brink of a breakdown here."

"Then eat your burger. Then you'll call him and give him the good news."

Meri picked up her burger, put it down again. "You know, it's not the 'Can I be a good mother to two teenagers,' or 'What if we get a divorce' stuff. It's just that he's waited so long to have his children with him, and I'm afraid that's what Nora's reacting to.

"Their relationship is fragile still, and adding me to the mix destroys that." She blew out a sigh. "I don't think I could stand that."

"Did you ask Nora?" Carlyn asked through a bite of burger.

"No. It never occurred to me until her announcement last night. I thought she was totally on board."

"Me, too."

Carlyn dunked an onion ring in catsup and handed it to Meri. "Maybe you should stop worrying about everybody else and think of yourself for a change."

"I am."

"Do you want to marry the guy or not?" She picked through the onion rings for the fattest one. "Because let me tell you. If you don't want him, I might just ask him out."

Meri tried not to smile. She needed to be serious. But she couldn't hold out against Carlyn's jackhammer techniques.

"He doesn't sing karaoke."

Carlyn sighed. "I could train him."

"Stop it."

"So what will it be? Yes I do. No I don't. Or you'll take what's behind door number three?

"I think Alden, Nora, and I should sit down and talk things out."

"That wouldn't be my first choice, but since you can't always get what you want, I think you should go for it."

Meri dug in her bag for her phone.

"But maybe not while 'Louie Louie' is playing in the background. He might get the wrong idea."

EVEN GRAN LOOKED worried, Nora thought as she watched her stir the stew she'd made that afternoon. She had helped, a little bit. Gran had taught her to cook a few things when she'd been trying to get her dad to let her stay.

He'd finally convinced her mom to let her come live with him, and now look where they were. She didn't understand why her dad hadn't just made Meri come home.

How he could be so complacent? No, that wasn't it. Usually when he was upset he went to sit on the rocks overlooking the bay. Or worked at his drawing table. But they were still at Gran's. It was almost like he was afraid to leave.

And that scared Nora. There had to be a way to make this right. If only she hadn't talked to Lucas, they'd probably all be having dinner together, laughing and talking about decorating and wedding flowers, and her Dad would pretend like he didn't get any of it but he would be happy. Like he'd been until a few days ago.

None of them said much while they ate. Gran kept glancing out the kitchen window like maybe she heard something. But it was just hope.

Meri didn't come.

"I think you should call her again," Nora said.

"It's her move," her dad said.

Nora cast a pleading look at Gran. She just shrugged and went back to picking at her apple cobbler.

They washed and dried the dishes like always. And Nora was thinking that she hoped they would still eat over here even after Mrs. Miller started cooking for them. Then she remembered, she might not even be here then. Meri and Dad might not be living together and she'd feel sick.

Even when they were walking home she knew her dad was looking out for Meri's car. She sure was. Once, she saw headlights out on the road, but they kept going and Nora slumped with disappointment. Her dad just kept walking.

He's like a zombie, she thought. Not the dragging leg kind of monsters that have books written about them, but the living dead. She gasped.

Her dad reached for her elbow. "Are you okay?"

She nodded, but she took his arm as if she could hold him there, keep him from going to that place that scared her, that made her sad, because she knew he was alone there. And she prayed that Meri would come home.

As soon as they got home she went to her room. Locked the door and pulled out her cell.

She texted Lucas. *Call me. Now.*

Nothing.

She couldn't wait. *Emergency.*

Nothing. She called him.

"What?" he said on the fourth ring.

"That's a terrible way to answer the phone."

"What do you want, I'm really busy." A pause. "It isn't Dad? Nothing's happened to Dad?"

"Nobody's dead, if that's what you mean. But we have a serious problem."

"Okay. Just hang on a minute so I can finish my . . ."

He left her to silence. She could hear him rummaging around in the background. Then he was back.

"Okay. What's the big emergency?"

"Meri's left."

"So? Where'd she go?"

"She went back to Newport, because she thinks we don't want her to marry Dad."

"Well, that's dumb. Why does she think that?"

"It's all your fault," Nora said, hoping it wasn't all her fault. And afraid that maybe it was.

"My fault? I'm not even there. I haven't talked to Meri since Thanksgiving."

"It's what you said about all those statistics and second marriages."

"What does that have to do with anything?"

"Are they true?"

"They're based on collected data and make certain assumptions after taking into account standard deviations."

"Speak English, dammit. This is serious."

"I am being serious."

"But will it happen to Meri and Dad?"

"What?"

"You said they would want to be alone so they could start their own family right away."

"I didn't."

"Your statistics did."

"Statistics are bodies of input, they're percentages."

"You mean Meri and Dad might not be that way."

"Yes. Or they might. It depends on a lot of factors. You said there was an emergency. Can you get to your point?"

"I called Mom and told her I wanted to move back to her house."

Nothing but nasal breathing from the other end. Finally, "Are you crazy? Why did you do that? You hate it there."

"I thought it would be better for Dad and Meri, and now everything is all screwed up. And I'm afraid there's not going to be a wedding."

"That was the dumbest thing."

"I know. I'm dumb. I get that."

"You're not dumb. You just think with your emotions. Not a good way to deal with things."

"Are you sure you're my brother? That brother is a nerdy kid but he's not some stuffy automaton with no emotions."

"I've got emotions. I'm just saying you shouldn't have had a knee jerk reaction."

"Well, I did, and you have to fix it."

"Nora, maybe we ought to leave it alone. They're the adults."

"Lucas. Help me fix this."

"Have any ideas?"

"No. You're the brainiac."

"With statistics. People? Not so much."

"Well, too bad. You started this, now figure out what we can do."

He huffed out a sigh. "Let me think. I'll get back to you."

"Okay, but don't go back to your books and forget."

"You think I would forget about Dad getting married?"

She really didn't know. Her brother was a kid and yet he sometimes sounded like some old geezer. "What do you want me to do?"

"Nothing. Don't do anything. I'll take care of it."

"How?"

"That's for me to figure out."

"You'd better hurry."

"I will, but Nora . . ."

"What?"

"Whatever happens, don't you dare run away."

Chapter 10

MERI WOKE TO hammering. At first she thought it was a hangover; she'd had two glasses of wine with Carlyn. Over her limit. She looked around, realized she was still in her apartment in Newport. Someone next door must be renovating or hanging pictures.

Newport. She grabbed for her phone. It past nine o'clock. She'd overslept.

And there was no message from Alden.

Maybe he didn't want to talk to her. She had really blown it.

She should have driven back last night. Except between the wine and the catharsis, Carlyn had convinced her it wouldn't be safe. That's when she'd had the second glass.

The hammering started up again.

"Oh, finish already," she said to no one in particular, and flopped back on her bed.

Why hadn't he called? He'd said it was her move. So she'd made it. Called and said she wanted to talk. Finished with "I love you. Call me." And hung up to wait.

She'd stayed up late waiting for Alden to return her call. She'd fallen asleep sometime during the night. She'd meant to get up early and drive home, and now she'd overslept.

She was a little worried that he hadn't called her back.

Her phone rang. And she exhaled in enormous relief.

She swiped her finger across the screen twice before it activated.

"Alden?"

"Uh, no."

"Who is this?" she asked.

"Lucas."

"Lucas?"

"Yeah, Lucas Corrigan."

"Where are you?" Had something happened to Alden?

"I'm outside your apartment. Where are you?"

"I'm inside my apartment. Have you been knocking?"

"Yes, persistently. I was afraid I'd missed you."

"I thought that was next door. Wait a minute, I'll let you in."

She dragged on the jeans she'd worn last night, exchanged her night shirt for a sweatshirt, shoved her feet into fur-lined moccasins, and hurried to let Lucas in.

It was a shock to see him. He'd been about her height at Thanksgiving, but now he looked even taller. Dark hair like his father's. Though cut short because of the school regulations. With the same pale complexion. He was so much like his dad, and for a moment she just looked at him, thinking of the boy not much younger than this who had saved her mother—and her—from a watery death.

"Come in; you must be freezing. How did you get here? Does your dad know? Did he send you?"

Lucas came in, slipped a heavy backpack from his shoulders and let it drop to the floor. "It's pretty cold out there. I got a ride from a kid and his parents who dropped me off on their way to Portsmouth. Dad doesn't know and he didn't send me."

Meri grinned. "I've missed you."

Lucas looked uncomfortable.

"Come on in. I don't have any food, are you hungry?"

"Yeah, but it can wait."

"That sounds serious. What's up? Why did you come here instead of going home? Did you get off a day early?"

Lucas unzipped his jacket, pulled it off, looked around for a place to put it. Meri took it from him and hugged it. It was very cold.

"How long were you waiting?"

"A few minutes. Listen." He turned to face her. "Nora called and said you and Dad were breaking it off."

"She did?"

"Yes. She seems to think it's her fault. Just because I told her about some stupid statistics. Sometimes she can be such a butthead."

"What kind of statistics?"

"The usual. The longevity of second marriages, but since it's your first—or I guess it is—the statistics will be skewed. And about the need to start a new family right away."

Enlightenment dawned. "And Nora was afraid she'd be replaced with a— What did she call Jennifer's new baby?"

"The little worm."

"Right. So she decided to go back to your mother before that happened? Honestly, did she think she could ever be replaced by someone else. Or you?" Meri added.

Lucas shrugged. But a slash of pink grew across his pale cheeks.

"Lucas, we would never do that. Even if—you know—we started— If we had—"

Lucas waved her aside. "Whatever."

Meri blushed. She had no idea how to talk about sex to a teenage boy. So they both stood looking at the floor until Lucas said, "So do you love my dad or not?"

"With all my heart."

"Then—"

"Lucas, I love your dad more than anything. But I don't have to marry him, if it makes you and Nora unhappy. We can just go along being the way we are now. It's fine. I understand. Besides, I'm not sure I can be helpful if you and Nora need to talk about anything."

"Talk about what?"

"You know, things you talk about with parents. I'm not sure I'd be all that good at it."

Lucas frowned. "Jeez, Meri. After our mother? You wouldn't have to be too good."

Meri's heart broke for both these neglected children, and she promised herself that even if she made a million mistakes, she would always make the time for them.

"What else?"

Meri frowned. "What do you mean?"

Lucas sighed. "You love my dad, you don't have to be a good mother, and Nora and I both want you to marry him, and—oh yeah—Nora wants to know if she can stay after all."

"Of course she can. You, too, if you decide you don't like boarding school."

"So we're solid?"

Meri nodded. "Yeah. We are."

"In that case . . ." Lucas knelt on one knee. "Will you, Meri Calder-Hollis, marry us, all of us, even when we're buttheads?"

Meri looked into that earnest face and nodded, though she found herself very close to tears. "I do. As long as you take me when I'm a butthead, too."

"I do. We all do." He stood. "Now can we eat? I didn't have time for breakfast before I left."

"Of course. Give me a second to get dressed. We'll have to go out. I don't have anything in the fridge. Then we'll drive out to the farm.

"Oh! I forgot. I have a dress fitting." She looked at the wall clock. "In less that an hour." She began looking for her purse. "Can you make do with a bagel from the deli? I'm sure Gran will make you a gigantic breakfast once we get home."

NORA LOOKED FROM Gran to Edie Linscott. Meri's wedding dress was hanging from the doortop, ready to be tried on.

But there was no Meri. And Nora hadn't heard from Lucas.

Gran glanced out the window. "I'm sure she'll be here any minute. She probably hit traffic getting out of Newport. Big tourist season at Christmas."

Gran sounded awfully sure that Meri would come.

They'd had breakfast earlier, though none of them ate very much. Her dad had tried to leave afterward, but Gran put him to work, chopping wood. She already had plenty of wood. Dad always made sure the woodpile was stocked.

But Nora thought she knew what Gran was doing. Giving him something to do until Meri came.

If she came. What if she never came back? Lucas said he would fix it. But he was only thirteen, and barely thirteen at that.

She'd have to go into Newport herself and ask Meri to come back. Explain to her why she'd said she was moving back with her mother. Ask Meri to give her a second chance, and then somehow she'd make Meri marry her dad.

She'd promised Lucas she wouldn't run away. She'd done that before. But she hadn't said she wouldn't drive away. She had her restricted license. She was pretty good with the SUV even though it was kind of big. She'd just drive to Newport.

Except that she didn't know how to park. She'd go to Gilbert House; they had a lot in back. But no one would be working there.

She'd go there and call Meri to pick her up. She wouldn't say no, would she? Except Meri was probably mad at her. Mad? She probably hated her for wrecking her wedding.

Nora bit her lip really hard so she wouldn't cry. She pulled out her cell. Still nothing from Lucas.

Mrs. Linscott lifted her eyebrows at Gran and they went into the other room.

Nora followed them to the door, heard Edie say, "Trouble in paradise?"

"A bit," Gran said. "Let's have a cup of coffee while we wait."

Nora went to the window. She'd looked out every few minutes since breakfast was over. She could hear her dad chopping wood like he wanted to kill it. He probably wished he could kill her.

She had to do something. They'd walked over and the SUV was in the garage. She could probably get home without him seeing her. And get the SUV started and onto the road before he could run after her. Of course there was the truck.

Though he'd probably just call the cops. Maybe even say she stole his car. They'd put her in jail. Fine. It couldn't be much worse than going back to New Haven.

"Oh stop exaggerating," she told herself. Why couldn't she be more like Lucas and not get into trouble all the time.

And then she saw it. Blinked. It was still there. The chopping outside had stopped. Her dad had seen it, too.

Meri had come back. That meant she'd come home for good. That the wedding would take place and then . . . It didn't matter as long as Meri and her dad got married.

She ran down the hall to the kitchen. Burst into the room. Gran and Mrs. Linscott looked up from the table where they were drinking coffee.

"She's here," Nora said, and kept going through the mudroom and out the back door.

Meri's car got closer and closer but it seemed to be going in slo-mo. Finally it turned into the drive and came to a stop at the farmhouse. Nora felt Gran and Mrs. Linscott come out behind her. She could see her dad at the corner of the house.

He just stood waiting. And Nora got it. He wasn't sure if she'd come back for real. *Please don't give up. Make her marry you.*

Slowly he came forward.

Two car doors opened. Two?

Meri got out of the driver's side and Lucas got out of the other one. He reached back in and hauled out his backpack.

He'd done it! He'd gotten her to come back. She could kiss him. If he weren't her brother.

Lucas and Meri walked toward the group side by side. Gran, Nora, and Alden moved closer together. Even Mrs. Linscott waited expectantly.

Lucas and Meri slowed a little as they got to the group.

Lucas stepped forward. Looked at his dad.

"Lucas? Where did you come from?" Alden asked.

"From school. Got a ride."

"Wha—"

"Dad, it's okay. It's a done deal. She said yes. To all of us." He shifted his backpack. "Gran, do you have time to make me some breakfast? I only had a bagel on the way out here."

"All the time in the world." Gran held out both arms. He allowed her to give him a quick hug and they went into the kitchen. Mrs. Linscott followed them in.

Nora started to go, too, but Meri called her back. Nora turned and hung her head. If it meant she had to go back to New Haven, she'd go. And she wouldn't cause any trouble there as penance. Well, not much.

"Look at me." Meri sounded stern. Nora looked at her.

"Don't even think about living anywhere else but with us. If I have to lock you in your room and shove a plate of old bread under the door for you to eat, you're staying with us."

Nora stared at her. She was going to stay. She couldn't believe it. They were getting married and she was going to stay. "I love old bread." She gave them both a quick hug, then ran after Gran and Lucas, calling, "Make extra for me. I'm starving."

"Whew," Alden said.

"I've been such a butthead," Meri said.

Alden raised both eyebrows.

"Lucas called us the butthead family. It was music to my ears."

"Well, you did give me a few sleepless nights."

"I called you last night. Why didn't you call me back?"

He shrugged. His arms had slipped around her. "I was afraid of what you were going to say."

"I told you I loved you."

"I know, but that was after you said we needed to talk."

"Well, we do. There are so many things to think about."

" 'We need to talk' is usually what women say when they're dumping you."

"Oh, Alden, you're—"

"Such a butthead."

She laughed, and he kissed her and they walked into the house to tell Gran to add more eggs to the pan. They were all starving this morning.

Chapter 11

FOR THE NEXT week, Corrigan House was overrun with decorators, caterers, and cleaning staff. Mrs. Miller turned out to be not only a good cook, who actually liked teenagers, but also a good organizer. And after a few days the household was running as smoothly as if she'd been there for years.

The Corrigans spent a good part of the days at the farmhouse, especially after Alden's drafting table had been moved to a storage room to make room for the buffet tables.

"We should have eloped," Alden groused, but nobody paid him any attention.

"They talk about a bride glowing," Gran said while she and Mrs. Linscott made the final adjustments to Meri's dress. "I don't think I've ever seen Alden so happy. Finally," she added under her breath.

Happy maybe, but nervous, Meri thought. She pushed

the thought away. No more waffling. She was getting married.

Nora went off to school every day, but not until she tried to finagle another sick day. Alden held firm and Meri backed him up. Even Gran told her to stop whining and get it done.

On Tuesday, Alden drove Lucas back to school to pick up some clothes and books since he'd only had time to shove some things into his backpack for his early morning trip to Meri's apartment.

On Thursday, Dan Hollis arrived, and so did Meri's three half brothers, one sister-in-law, and a baby. They all crammed into Gran's farmhouse like the old days.

Only one was missing.

On the day before the wedding, Meri asked Gran to take her to the cemetery. It was early morning when they carefully picked their way over the frozen snow toward the Calder plot. Meri held Gran tightly by the arm. Not just giving her support over the uneven ground, but receiving it in turn.

It was an old cemetery next to the church. Many of the graves were old, well-tended by the church but forgotten by their ancestors, if indeed there were any left.

The large granite monument of the first Calder was flanked by two fir trees, planted several years before and decorated with red ribbons and tiny silver bells. To either side, the markers of Calders from several generations were covered in blankets of pine.

"Gran, you did all this?"

Gran nodded. She'd stopped at the marker of her

husband, Cyrus, and Meri stepped away to give her time alone with her love.

Meri continued on to the three graves that sat side by side. Her mother, Laura Calder-Hollis, the woman who had raised her and loved her for her entire life. Her mother, Riley, the young teenage girl who had left Meri in Laura's care.

And between them the baby that was not to grow up and reap the wonders of being part of such a loving family. Meri took a moment to acknowledge them all, then stood at her mother's feet. Felt Gran come up beside her.

"She always hoped you and Alden would build a life together."

"She never said anything."

"What we hope for and what we get isn't always the same thing. We all knew that if it was meant to be, the two of you would figure it out."

"I wish she could be here."

"Oh, she'll be there," Gran said. "Have no doubt about that. They'll all be there. Because you're a Calder first and foremost, and a Hollis, and soon to be a Corrigan. Now let's get back home, before the boys ransack the kitchen in search of sustenance."

The "boys" had left a note. They'd gone out for breakfast. Penny and baby Laura were still asleep.

"Well, a little peace and quiet," Gran said, though Meri knew she'd enjoyed every loud bustling minute of having her entire family under her roof, as well as the Corrigans, for most of their waking hours.

"Nope," came a voice from the kitchen door. "You got me."

"Nora," Gran said. "Are you playing hooky?"

"No. Dad and the school gave me a dispensation because of the wedding. Besides, Carlyn is coming out and we're trying on our dresses and accessorizing. Oh, and Geordie asked if it was okay if she came and got some candid day-before shots." Nora grinned. "I said sure."

"The more the merrier," Gran said. "Though I'd better check the pantry."

Meri made more coffee. The back door opened. Alden walked in and tossed his coat on a hook.

"I've been thrown out of my house. I guess I was taking up too much room. One more poinsettia and I'll go off to bedlam and you and Nora can sell them on the street corner to pay for my room and board."

"The Little Match Girl?" Meri asked.

Nora laughed. "La Belle et Le Bête. And we know which one beauty is." She strutted around, casting saucy looks back at her father.

Meri marveled at how fast she had rebounded from miserable unloved teenager to Madame Provocateur.

"Well, it's a toss-up between you and Meri. And Gran," he added as she come out of the pantry.

"Gran what?" she asked.

"Is a beauty." Nora gave her a big hug.

"Watch the pasta," Gran said.

Nora pulled back. "Pasta? What are we making?"

"Lasagna. It's easy and I have pans big enough to feed this whole crowd."

"Oh good, I've never made lasagna before."

Alden took the opportunity to pull Meri into the mudroom. Took a quick look into the kitchen to make sure Nora and Gran were busy and kissed her. "Want to go make out in the back seat of my SUV?"

"What?" Meri asked, laughing.

"It's the only place where there aren't people."

"I know, but you have to admit, it's pretty cool."

He sighed. "Yeah, and the kids are really liking it. Dan came by and asked Lucas to go with them to the deli, and Lucas actually closed his book and went. Wonder of wonders. Though I wouldn't mind a little quiet time."

"Me too, but don't hold your breath. Look who just drove up."

Carlyn's old sports car pulled up to the back door. Carlyn jumped out and ran around the side to open the passenger door. She began to lug out equipment, which was finally followed by Geordie Holt, karaoke partner and dynamite photographer, who would be taking photos of the wedding. They lugged the equipment inside.

"Better put all that stuff upstairs in my room," Meri said. "We're wall-to-wall people here. But try to be quiet; mama and baby are still sleeping."

"Baby is, mama is not." Penny Hollis yawned from the doorway then padded over to Gran and gave her a kiss. "Is there coffee?" She ended the question with a big yawn. "Sorry, the baby got overexcited last night with all the attention; she kept waking up all night long. Tonight we both go to bed early."

Gran left the lasagna preparations and moved to the

coffeepot. "You sit down and I'll make you breakfast. Meri and I haven't had a proper breakfast, and I bet you haven't either, Nora."

"Mrs. Miller wanted to make me oatmeal but I wanted to get over here."

"Don't you dare let Mrs. Miller think you like Gran's cooking better than hers," Alden said, then shrugged at Gran. "We do. But we don't want to hurt her feelings and we don't want her to quit."

Meri sighed happily. She'd never seen Alden so playful, well, not in a long, long time. She knew it wouldn't always be this way, he was "deep," as Gran would say. He could be moody and distant. But Meri knew all his moods and he knew hers. She was ready. She knew that now. She was really ready.

Alden and Carlyn pulled extra chairs around the kitchen table while Meri got eggs and Canadian bacon out of the fridge. Gran laid a towel over the lasagna preparations and got two cast-iron pans out of the cupboard and placed them on the stove. Meri made more coffee while Geordie took photos.

Breakfast was a rowdy affair, with baby Laura, awaken by all the commotion, adding her voice to theirs, and Alden took off as soon as he finished.

"Poor man," Gran said. "I do believe his solitary days are over."

"Okay, everybody squeeze in," Geordie said. "We'll do a three generation shot of Calder Hollis Corrigan women."

"Cool." Nora looked around. She was beaming.

It was pretty special, Meri thought, proud and humble and so happy that this family had made her theirs. Only Gran seemed a little subdued, and Meri guessed she was thinking of her daughter and husband gone and still missed. Meri put her arm around her.

"Love you, Gran."

"Love you, too." And the faraway look receded and she smiled with the others.

"Can I hold baby Laura?" Nora asked Penny.

"Absolutely." Penny handed the squirming infant to Nora, who held her up before settling her on her lap. Laura gurgled and Nora laughed.

Her eye caught Meri's. "It might be fun to have a little sister."

Everyone looked at Meri.

Meri laughed. "But what if you got a brother instead?"

Nora shrugged. "I would be okay, I guess." She tickled Laura's chin and the baby laughed.

Meri breathed out a sigh of relief. There was plenty of time to think about a bigger family down the road. For now, she planned to enjoy the one she would be joining tomorrow.

Chapter 12

The marriage of Merielle Calder-Hollis and Alden William Corrigan took place on Saturday at the groom's home, Corrigan House, in Little Compton in front of a gathering of thirty family members and friends.

MERI TOOK TWO deep breaths.

"Nervous?" Carlyn asked.

"A bit. Excited. I hope I don't fall down the stairs. Why did I ever say I'd make my entrance like that? I must have been crazy."

"It will be good for a photo op," Geordie said, and fired off a couple of shots of Meri's dress. "Which reminds me, I'd better get downstairs and claim my place." She paused, looked at Meri and smiled. "You're really beautiful."

When the door closed behind her, Meri asked, "Do you think she wants to get married? She met Bruce less than a year ago."

"I think we're all just a little in awe of the whole event," Carlyn said.

"I am," Nora confessed. "I'm nervous, too."

There was a knock at the door.

"This better not be the bridegroom," Carlyn said through the door.

"Nope, father of the bride."

Carlyn opened the door. Dan Hollis stopped just over the threshold. "Oh, my."

"Oh no, not you, too," Carlyn said. "Have a tissue."

"Happy tears," Dan said. "Seeing you in that dress . . . it's just perfect."

Meri touched the locket she wore around her neck. Dan had given it to her on her thirtieth birthday, the same night she'd learned she wasn't actually a Calder at all. But she was. In everything that counted, love, support, acceptance, she was a Calder and a Hollis, and soon a Corrigan.

"It's time to go."

Nora and Carlyn exchanged looks, then turned to Meri.

"See you downstairs." Carlyn pecked the air near Meri's cheek.

"I'm holding onto the banister going down," Nora said, and gave her a quick kiss on the other cheek.

"We both are."

"I'm holding onto dad." Meri said.

The bride wore a full length wedding dress of pearl satin and vintage lace, a Calder family heirloom, and carried a bouquet of blush roses and white baby orchids. She was accompanied by two bridesmaids,

*Nora Elyse Corrigan and Carlyn Anderson. Both
bridesmaids wore tea length dresses of deep bur-
gundy. A string quartet played as they descended
the wide walnut staircase that was lined with pots
of white poinsettias.*

Nora was feeling all jittery. But not angry, not afraid;
just excited. Change was good, she thought as she stepped
off the last step and started down the aisle between the
rental chairs and the crowd of family and friends and her
dad's editors. But they all went out of focus when she saw
her father, not smiling exactly, but looking so handsome
in his tuxedo that Nora thought he should draw himself
as the fairy prince.

Even Lucas, who was the best man—the idea made her
smile—looked good in his new tuxedo. And so grown-up.

She managed not to race down the aisle, but walked
sedately to her place. Carlyn came behind her, then they
both turned to give Gran a kiss where she was sitting in
the front row.

*The bride was given away by her father, Daniel
Hollis, of Hartford, Connecticut.*

"Here we go," Dan said when the quartet began the
wedding march. "Your mother would be so happy."

Meri nodded. She didn't dare speak. She felt like she
might burst into tears, overflowing with awe and excitement.

She made it down the stairs without tripping and took

it as a good omen, though it seemed to take forever to walk through the guests toward the massive Christmas tree that towered over the preacher and wedding party.

She could hear Geordie's camera whirring away. Caught Doug's eye as she passed. He was grinning from ear to ear, now that she had assured him she wouldn't be leaving the crew once she was married.

Next to him Joe Krosky looked civilized and quite handsome in his suit and tie and slicked back hair. She could see his knee bouncing as she walked by.

She paused to smile at her other father, Everett Simmons, and his wife Inez. A father Meri had only known for a few short months; the boy who had loved a teenage girl and was responsible for her existence.

In the first row, her brothers and Penny—who had left baby Laura with Mrs. Miller in the kitchen—smiled broad smiles. Gran gave her an encouraging nod and Meri's eyes filled, overwhelmed by the love and gratitude she felt for them all.

And finally they reached the preacher. Carlyn took her bouquet; her father kissed her and stepped away. Alden took his place and they became the only two people in the room.

And they were married. Meri managed not to cry, but the vows passed in a dream, and before she knew it she was wearing a wedding ring and Alden was kissing her. And she kissed him back.

The recessional music struck up, and she would have kept kissing him if everyone hadn't stood and begun applauding.

It made her laugh. And when the two of them walked back up the aisle, there were several cheers and more than one amen rising from the group.

The couple will divide their time between Newport, where the bride works as an architectural restorer, and Corrigan House, where the groom is a book illustrator.

Since the reception was in the next room, they had decided to forgo the formal receiving line, but made themselves available to those who were from out of town and not staying for the festivities.

"Congratulations." Gabe Hollis, Penny's husband, shook Alden's hand. "We thought we'd never get rid of her."

Meri made a face at him.

"You looked a little nervous at first. Worried about getting hitched to my crazy sister?"

"More worried that I wouldn't get hitched to your crazy sister," Alden said.

Meri gave his arm a squeeze.

"Nah, we wouldn't let her get away."

"Gabe! Behave," Penny said, and smacked him in the arm.

"Silly boy," Gran said. She turned to Alden with a smile that spoke volumes.

Alden leaned over and hugged her, a long hug. So long that Meri had to nudge him to tell him that Everett Simmons and his wife Inez were taking their leave.

After they had shaken hands and kissed Meri, Dan Hollis walked them out to their car.

Geordie insisted on getting a few shots in front of the sea, so the wedding party and Geordie and Bruce Stafford donned coats and went outside.

"Don't worry about the goose bumps, girls," Bruce said. "Geordie can photo shop them out."

"Very funny," Geordie said, but she wasn't annoyed. The two of them had gotten off to a rough start when Geordie first came to work for the project. She lacked experience and it turned out she was a much better people photographer. Since then they'd become good friends. Maybe more than friends, Meri thought, listening to their banter.

When they came back inside, Carlyn and Nora called for Meri to throw her bouquet. So she climbed halfway up the staircase and looked back over her shoulder.

All the girls crowded forward, except Carlyn. Until Joe Krosky pushed her toward the group at the same time Alden extricated Nora, who had been standing front and center.

That set off a burst of laughter, and Meri threw the bouquet over her shoulder, then turned to see who caught it. It was arcing toward Carlyn but she stepped aside at the last minute and it landed in Geordie's hands.

Geordie laughed and shook her head. But Meri noticed she glanced at Bruce and he didn't look away.

Meri came back down the stairs. Her feet were beginning to hurt, and since almost all the nonfamily and close friend guests had left, she kicked off her shoes and made her way over to Carlyn and Krosky.

"How come you didn't try to catch the bouquet?" Meri asked, teasing. Carlyn liked serial dating.

"Heck, what if I caught it and it came true? You'd miss me at karaoke night."

Krosky bounced on his toes. "Not if the guy you married liked to sing, too." He grinned.

Carlyn rolled her eyes.

Krosky just kept grinning and bouncing.

When the last of the guests had driven away, the Hollises bundled up and walked across the dunes to the farmhouse. Nora and Lucas had changed into comfortable clothes and taken a tray of food up to the new and improved television and game room.

The chairs were folded and carried away, the furniture restored to its natural place in an efficient slight of hand. Alden took off his jacket and untied his tie. Carlyn had long since zipped Meri out of the wedding dress, and she'd changed into a soft knit sweater dress and bedroom slippers.

The two of them sat on the couch looking up at the tree framed by the French doors and the night beyond.

A bottle of champagne sat between them on the floor.

Alden took her hand. "Are you sure you don't want to go on a honeymoon?"

"I'm sure."

"I just don't want you to regret anything down the road."

"I won't."

"You're sure?"

"Oh Alden, don't be a butthead. We are already at the perfect place for us."

"You learned that from Lucas and Nora, didn't you?"

"From the best," she said.

"In that case, my love, welcome home." And he kissed her.

Continue reading for a sneak peek at
Shelley Noble's next fantastic beach read

Whisper Beach

Fifteen years ago, seventeen-year-old Vanessa Moran fell in love and lost her virginity—but not to the same boy. Pregnant, desperate, and humiliated, she fled friends and family and Whisper Beach, New Jersey. She hasn't been back since. Now a professional Manhattan organizer, she returns to the funeral of her best friend's husband. She means to pay her respects, let the town see the successful businesswoman she's become, and get the hell out. But her girlfriends have other ideas.

Dorie, the owner of the pier's Blue Crab Restaurant, where Van and her friends worked as teenagers, needs help. The restaurant is failing, since Dorie's roving husband manages to spend every penny they make. Joe, the boy Van left behind without an explanation, has never stopped loving her. And he's cautiously interested in seeing what would happen if they took up where they left off. But he doesn't know Van's secret and the reason she fled without a word.

As the summer progresses and the restaurant takes on a new look, trouble comes from unexpected sources, and the friends must reevaluate their own lives and their loyalty to each other. For Van, this summer will test the meaning of friendship, the boundaries of trust, and just how far love can bend before it breaks.

Coming Summer 2015

for just a second. Gigi looked older than she... no, she'd gained weight. And now she was a widow.

Her cousin Gigi. Practically the same age, and best friends from the first time you'd put of the centaurs of her shiny top over Vanessa's dark hair. Vanessa didn't remember the incident, but that's what they told her. Of course you could hardly trust anything the Moran sort of

VANESSA MORAN WAS wearing black. Of course she always wore black; she was a New Yorker . . . and it was a funeral. She'd dressed meticulously (she always did), fashionable but respectful, chic but not different enough to call attention to herself.

Still, for a betraying instant, standing beneath the sweltering August sun, the gulls wheeling overhead and promising cool salt water nearly within reach, she longed for a pair of faded cutoffs and a T-shirt with some tacky slogan printed across the front.

She shifted her weight, and her heels sank a little lower in the soil. The sweat began to trickle down her back. She could feel her hair beginning to curl. She should have left after Mass, sneaked out of the church before anyone recognized her.

But what would be the point of that?

When she saw Gigi sitting bolt upright in that front pew, Van suddenly felt the weight of the years, the guilt, the sadness, the—and by the time she'd roused herself, the pallbearers were already moving the casket down the aisle.

She bowed her head while her cousin and, at one time, best friend passed by, but she couldn't resist glancing up

for just a second. Gigi looked older than she should; she'd gained weight. And now she was a widow.

Her cousin, Gigi. Practically the same age, and best friends from the first time Gigi poured the contents of her sippy cup over Vanessa's curly hair. Vanessa didn't remember the incident, but that's what they told her. Of course you could hardly trust anything the Moran side of her family said.

And Van knew she couldn't leave without at least paying her condolences. Wasn't that really why she'd come? To make her peace with the past. Then let it go.

So she followed the others across the street to the cemetery, stood on the fringes of the group, looking across the flower-covered casket to where her cousin stood between her parents. Gigi leaned against her father, Van's uncle Nate, the best of the Moran clan. On her other side, Aunt Amelia stood stiffly upright. Strong enough for two—or three.

Behind them the Morans, the Gilpatricks, the Dalys, and the Kirks stood clumped together, the women looking properly sad in summer dresses, the men in various versions of upright—nursing hangovers from the two-day wake—wilting inside their suit jackets.

The one person Van didn't see was her father. And that was fine by her.

Gigi, whose real name was Jennifer, was the good girl of the family. Except for the sippy cup incident, she'd always done the right thing. Boring but loyal, which Vanessa had reason to know and appreciate, Gigi was now a widow at thirty-one. It hardly seemed fair.

Then again, what in life was fair?

Van passed a hand over her throat. It came away wet with sweat. This was miserable for everyone, including the priest who was fully robed and standing in the sun in the middle of a New Jersey heat wave.

He opened his hands. It was a gesture all priests used, one that Vanessa had never understood. Benediction or surrender? In this case it could go either way.

" . . . et Spiritus Sancti . . ."

Vanessa lowered her head but watched the mourners through her lashes. In the glare of the sun it was hard to distinguish faces. But she knew them. Most of them.

"I wondered if you'd show."

Vanessa's head snapped around.

"Shh. No squealing or kissing and hugging."

"Suze? What are you doing here?"

Suzanne Turner was the only person Van had kept in touch with since leaving Whisper Beach. And that had been sporadic at best. She hadn't actually seen Suze in years. But she was the same Suze, tall and big-boned, expensively but haphazardly dressed in a sleeveless gray sheath and a voile kimono. A college professor, she looked fit enough to wrestle any recalcitrant student into appreciating Chaucer.

Suze leaned closer and whispered, "Same reason you're here. Dorie called me."

"And where is she?"

"Probably over at the pub setting up the reception. She demands your presence."

Vanessa closed her eyes. "I suppose I have to go."

"Damn straight. Dorie said if you sneaked out again without saying good-bye, she'd—and I quote—follow your skinny ass to wherever and give you what for."

Vanessa snorted. Covered it over with a cough when several disgruntled mourners turned to give her the evil eye.

"Let us pray."

Suze pulled her back a little ways from the group. She was trying not to laugh. Which would be a disaster. Suze had a deep belly laugh that could attract crowds.

Vanessa lowered her voice. "How does she know I have a skinny ass? For all she knows I could have gained fifty pounds in the last twelve years."

Suze glanced down at Vanessa's butt. "But you didn't. Did you ever think that maybe Doric is clairvoyant?"

Vanessa rolled her eyes. She certainly hoped not. She moved closer to Suze, gingerly lifting her heels out of the soil.

"A bitch on shoes, these outdoor funerals," Suze said. "You look great by the way. You're bound to wow whoever might be here and interested."

Van narrowed her eyes at Suze. "How long have you been here? Who else is here?"

"I don't know. I just got a cab from the station. The train was late and I was afraid I'd miss the whole thing. Changed clothes in the parish office. Nice guy, this Father Murphy."

Another snort from Vanessa. She couldn't help it. "You're kidding. His name is Murphy? Really?" Every Sunday her father would drop her mother and her off

at the church with a "Going over to Father Murphy's for services. I'll pick you up afterwards." Mike Murphy owned the pub two blocks from the church. Mike was short on sermons, but his bar was well stocked and all his parishioners left happy.

Seemed nothing much had changed in Whisper Beach. They'd be going to the other Father Murphy's as soon as Clay Daly was laid to rest.

"In the name of . . ."

It was inevitable that some one would recognize her. As the amen died away and eyes opened, one pair rested on hers. Van stood a little straighter, lifted her chin. Pretended that her confidence wasn't slipping.

There was a moment of question, then startled recognition, a turn to his neighbor and the news rippled through the circle of mourners like a breeze off the river.

Van helplessly watched it make its way all the way to the family until it hit Gigi full force. Van could see her startle from where she was standing. The jerk of her head, the searching eyes. Van stepped farther back from the crowd and wedged herself between Suze and the Farley Mausoleum.

It was a desperate but futile attempt. Gigi found her and almost as one the entire family, the Morans, the Gilpatricks, the Dalys, and the Kirks, turned in her direction.

"Busted," Suze whispered.

"This is exactly what I didn't want to happen," Van whispered back.

"Then you should have come earlier and made your

condolences . . . before the public arrived. You can't expect them not to be curious. It's been twelve years, and half of the people here thought you were dead."

Suze was right. She could have called. Warned them she was coming. Asked if she would even be welcome. She hadn't.

She wasn't even sure why she had come, except that everything had coalesced at once. Her staff had been urging her to take a vacation. Dorie's letter had arrived at the same time. And Van thought what the hell; she blocked out two weeks of her schedule, made reservations at a four-star hotel in Rehoboth Beach, and got out her funeral dress.

Even once she'd packed, dressed, and picked up the rental car, she was still deliberating. She almost drove straight past the parkway exit to Whisper Beach. But in the end she'd come.

She'd known Gigi had gotten married. She'd even sent a gift. But without a return address. Maybe Gigi was relieved not to have to write a thank-you note.

Van had called her once after she left, just to let Gigi know she was all right. Gigi begged her to come home, but Van couldn't, even if she'd wanted to. And couldn't explain why.

How could she tell Gigi that she was living in an apartment with way too many people, most of them strangers. That she was afraid. Hurt. Angry. Sick. For a long time. That she'd nearly died before she caved and called Suze—not Gigi—for help.

Gigi had already done enough. Cleaned out her bank

account to help Van get away. Almost two thousand dollars, her college savings—all stolen while Van slept on the train ride to Manhattan.

"I'm beginning to think I shouldn't have come at all."

"Don't worry. The worst is over."

Oh no it wasn't. Van only hoped that she would be gone before the worst reared his ugly head.

"Well, you can't leave now. Everyone has seen you. Besides, I didn't have time for breakfast and I'm starving."

Gigi passed by, still supported by her father on one side and her mother on the other. Amelia was the only one who looked toward Van and Suze. And Van knew in that instant that regardless of the twelve years that had passed, she hadn't been forgiven.

"I'm not sure I can do this."

"You can and you will." Suze took her by the elbow and force-marched her toward the street. "We're both going. We're going to say our condolences to Gigi. Say hello to Dorie, eat, and then we can leave."

"I thought it would feel great to come back successful, independent, and well dressed. But now I'm thinking they'll hate me for it. I'm out of place here. What was I thinking? I won't be welcome. I know Aunt Amelia wishes I hadn't come."

"She's one person. And quite frankly, do you really care? You've come to pay your respects, and if they get the added benefit of seeing the success you've made of your life, well, good for you." Suze grinned.

Van couldn't help giving her an answering smile. It would be nice for everyone to know she'd survived. That

she'd made something of herself. And maybe she did have a few things to answer for. To some people. Not all. There were some people she would never forgive.

She'd left a lot of unfinished business here. She'd begun to think it could stay unfinished, but standing here, being back even for an hour, drove home how impossible that was. Maybe it was time she just got it done.

She turned abruptly and started around the back of the church.

"Hold up, where are you going?"

"I'm staying out of sight until the last possible moment."

"And make a grand entrance?"

"God, no. We're going in the back way."

JOE ENTHORPE SAT at the bar in Mike's Pub, nursing a beer he didn't want and would be too early to drink if he was just getting out of bed instead of finishing up a long ten hours of night fishing.

He knew he was stupid to come to Mike's knowing that Clay Daly's funeral repast would be in the party room down the hall. He hadn't gone to the funeral. Wouldn't have gone even if he hadn't been out all night. Still, he couldn't stay away.

The door opened, and the first of the mourners came in. He probably should say his condolences, but he smelled like sweat, beer, and fish. Better he just went home.

He ordered another beer.

Mike just slowly shook his head and slid a mug of

Guinness in his direction. Seems like today everybody remembered the summer he crashed and burned. Most of it took place right here at Mike's, before Mike kicked Van out for being underage.

The trouble with living in a place all your life—people didn't forget shit.

He plunked down a twenty and headed for the door.

"I'm guessing this ain't a big tip," Mike called after him. "I'll keep your change till you come back for it." Mike's laugh was the last thing Joe heard before he stepped out into the blinding sun.

DORIE LISTER WAS in the caterer's kitchen at the pub when she heard the first mourners arrive. They'd left their sadness at the door and were ready to eat, drink, and if not be totally merry, at least have a good time. Best way to mourn your dead was to send them off with a party.

Rumor was, Gigi didn't have a penny to her name. Nate and Amelia had to pay the funeral expenses, including the wake before the funeral and the repast after it. So Dorie had offered the catering services of the Blue Crab, free of charge. It was the least she could do. So what if she had to scrimp.

She dismissed the two girls who'd helped with the setup and sent them back to the restaurant to set up for dinner. It was the last Saturday of the season, and there would be a handful of tourists to be fed.

She pulled her cell phone out of her apron pocket. Something she had been doing all day. She'd gotten the

message from Suze that she was on her way. Nothing from Van. She wasn't surprised, but she was disappointed. Fool that she was, even after all these years, she'd expected Van to come.

Things had begun to unravel for Whisper Beach all those years ago. And it hadn't stopped. Maybe it wouldn't. Maybe she'd just have to sit back and watch all those young lives swirl right down the drain.

It was already too late for the likes of her, but she'd made her bed a long time ago. And all in all, it wasn't such a bad place to sleep.

Dorie dropped the phone back in her pocket, grabbed a hot pad, and pulled a tray of freshly browned Italian bread slices out of the oven. She placed the pan on a trivet and was just reaching for the bowl of tomato bruschetta when the door to the hall opened and Kippie Fuller slipped in and closed the door behind her.

"What? Out of shrimp bites already?"

Kippie shook her head. "You'll never guess who I think I saw at the funeral."

Kippie was big and moved slow, but she had a quick eye for gossip.

"Who?"

"I'm pretty sure it was her."

Dorie began to feel a glimmer of—not hope—exactly, but interest. Yes, interest, nothing more. She waited for Kippie to expound on the subject. She would; she always did.

"I didn't get a good look, but Pete Daly said it was her."

"Huh." Dorie untied her apron and threw it on the

counter. Patted her hair, freshly blond from Lucille over at Sea Breeze Beauty.

"Well, don't you want to know?"

"Sure." Dorie checked her lipstick in the coffee urn. Smacked her lips a couple of time.

"Robbie Moran's daughter. What's her name."

"You mean Vanessa?"

"Yes, that's the one. The one who ran off and left her daddy alone, poor man."

Short memories, Dorie thought.

"Poor soul, I hear he's pretty bad off."

"Kippie, Robbie Moran was born bad off and went downhill from there. And he brought it all on himself."

"The idea of her coming back after letting everybody think she was dead all these years."

Nobody who bothered to look for her, thought Dorie.

"Whole family's a little wacko if you ask me. Including that daughter of his. She's got her nerve showing up like this. There'll be trouble. You mark my words."

About the Author

SHELLEY NOBLE is a former professional dancer and choreographer. She most recently worked on the films *Mona Lisa Smile* and *The Game Plan*. She is a member of Sisters in Crime, Mystery Writers of America, and Romance Writers of America.

www.shelleynoble.com

Discover great authors, exclusive offers, and more at hc.com.